$\mathcal{K}$eep walking," B whispered. "Don't let Trina see us staring at her car."

The sedan turned onto the street and passed them, its engine barely making a sound.

"That car has a *professional* driver," George said. "A guy in a suit and one of those chauffeur hats."

"S'pose she's a princess?" B asked.

"I know; when have you ever seen a kid picked up from school by a chauffeur in a limo?"

B shook her head. "Never."

"Maybe she's not a princess," George conceded, "but it's a mystery, just the same."

DISCOVER ALL THE MAGIC!

B Magical

The Cat-Astrophe

By Lexi Connor

SCHOLASTIC INC.

New York   Toronto   London   Auckland
Sydney   Mexico City   New Delhi   Hong Kong

No part of this publication may be reproduced, stored in a retrieval system, or transmitted in any form or by any means, electronic, mechanical, photocopying, recording, or otherwise, without written permission of the publisher. For information regarding permission, write to Working Partners Limited, Stanley House, St. Chad's Place, London WC1X 9HH, United Kingdom.

ISBN 978-0-545-26553-9

Copyright © 2010 by Working Partners Ltd.
Series created by Working Partners Ltd., London
All rights reserved. Published by Scholastic Inc.,
557 Broadway, New York, NY 10012.
SCHOLASTIC, APPLE PAPERBACKS, and associated logos are trademarks and/or registered trademarks of Scholastic Inc.

12 11 10 9 8 7 6 5 4 3   11 12 13 14 15 16/0

Printed in the U.S.A.   40
This edition first printing, May 2011

Special thanks to Julie Berry

To David

Chapter 1

B's paintbrush hovered over the rough paper tacked to her easel. With the faintest of strokes, she trailed the tips of the bristles in a graceful arc.

Perfect.

Another whisker for Nightshade, her cat.

Only about twenty more to go.

With an apron tied around her waist and a spare paintbrush stuck in her ponytail, Beatrix, or "B" for short, glanced at the photo of her black tomcat pinned to the corner of the easel, dipped her brush in black paint, and carefully sketched another whisker.

Miss Willow, B's art teacher, strolled around the room. "Nice job, B," she said as she passed B's easel.

"Thanks," B said, quite pleased with how her masterpiece was turning out. She just couldn't stop thinking of black cats. The Black Cats were B's favorite band, and B was going to see them this Saturday live in concert.

"Quit humming, Bumble*bee*," Jason Jameson said. "You sound like a beehive, and you're giving the rest of us a headache."

B glowered at Jason, who'd been a raging pest ever since preschool. Now they were in sixth grade, and he was even worse. She hadn't realized she was humming as she painted, but that didn't mean she was going to let Jason Jameson have the last word. He and his insect insults, reserved specially for B, drove her buggy.

"What's the matter, don't you like the song?" B said, pretending to sound innocent. "I thought everyone liked the Black Cats."

"Was that 'Yowl' you were humming?" Jamal Burns asked. "That's their newest song."

"I bet that'll be the first song they play on Saturday," Kim Silsby said. "I'm so jealous that you get to go, B. You'll have to tell us everything about the concert."

B grinned. "I'm only going because George is the best friend ever." He'd won the tickets by coming in first in their English class's spelling bee and shared one of his tickets with B. "I can't wait until Saturday night."

"You're not the only one with tickets, Cockroach," Jason scoffed. "My parents bought me a seat in the second row. Betcha don't know how much that cost!"

"Who cares what it cost? Quit showing off, Jason," Kim said and turned back to B. "Don't you and George have front-row tickets?"

"Yes," B said, almost unable to contain her excitement. Her smile stretched so big her face almost hurt.

"Front row!" Jamal interjected. "Man, you're so lucky. You'll get to see the color of their eyes. Maybe even what they had for dinner."

"Ew, *gross*!" B laughed. She couldn't wait until Saturday to see her favorite band and her first real rock concert. It was like Christmas, Easter, the Fourth of July, Halloween, and her birthday all rolled into one.

"*Students*," Miss Willow interrupted. "Please! No chitter-chatter. Everyone back to their work."

B's classmates slipped behind their easels. B carefully painted another whisker, and then another, peering at the photograph between strokes to get each one perfect.

She was on her second-to-last one when Miss Willow's voice made her jump, causing B to drag her brush across Nightshade's face and smear one of his amber-colored eyes.

"Everyone," her art teacher said in an extra-cheery voice, "I have an announcement to make."

B groaned. Her painting was ruined! Here was where a little spot of magic would come in handy. Checking quickly to see that no one was looking at her easel, B whispered, "E-R-A-S-E." The black smudge disappeared, as B had known it would — but so did all the whiskers she'd added that morning. B sighed. It was typical of B's special brand of magic.

When she spelled words, things happened, but not always the things she had in mind.

"For heaven's sake, don't paint all over your-selves, Dustin and Jake! Now, class," Miss Willow said in that same extrasweet voice, "I want you all to meet a new student in our school, just joining us today. Her name is Katrina Lang."

B forgot her ruined painting and peered around her easel once more. There, next to Miss Willow's cluttered desk, stood a shy-looking girl in a dark skirt and a cream-colored sweater, very trim and proper except for her dark hair, which was pulled back into a messy bun. She wore thick-rimmed glasses that pointed upward at the corners — cat's eyes, B's mother had called them once at a costume shop. The kind of glasses people wore when B's mom was young. She had a green-and-pink plaid backpack slung over one shoulder. *She looks original, like a one-of-a-kind painting in a museum,* B thought.

"I hope you'll all make Katrina feel welcome here in our school," Miss Willow continued.

"What a *nerd*!" Jason whispered to Jenny Springbranch, who tittered softly. Katrina looked up briefly from staring at her shoes, her jaw set in a hard line. It was only for a split second, but B felt sure the new girl had heard what Jason said, even from all the way across the room.

Miss Willow steered Katrina toward the corner where B was working, and clipped a fresh piece of paper to the empty easel beside B. "Beatrix, will you show Katrina where the paints are kept, and help her find the supplies she needs? Katrina, we're painting animal portraits today." Miss Willow headed back to her desk, praising students' artwork as she went.

"Her name may be *Kat*-trina," Jason whispered loudly to Jenny, "but she looks more like a mouse to me. Hey, *Kat*-trina!" His freckle-plastered face broke into a nasty grin. "Why doncha paint a mouse self-portrait?"

Katrina's jaw set in a hard line once more. B steered her toward the back counter where the paints were kept. "Just ignore him," B said. "That's

Jason Jameson. He's like that to almost everyone. Don't worry, though. Most people here are nice."

Katrina studied B's face for a minute, her dark green eyes wary and doubtful.

"Here, let's fill your paint tray," B said. "What animal are you going to paint?"

"A panther," Katrina said without hesitation.

"Excellent!" B said. "Here's the bottle of black."

Katrina filled her tray with black paint, a little white, and a splash of yellow, while B got her a supply of brushes, an apron, and a cup of water.

"Thanks, Beatrix," Katrina said, this time with a warm smile.

"Not a problem. Call me 'B.'"

"Okay." Katrina grinned. "Call me 'Trina.'"

"Trina. I like that."

"For that matter," Trina added, "call me anything but late for dinner."

B laughed. *Wow, she's a different person when she's relaxed.*

They returned to their workstations. Jason Jameson grabbed bottles of green and orange paint, squirted way too much of it into the tray on his easel, and bumped into B's easel accidentally-on-purpose after returning the bottles to the back counter.

"Out of my way, Stinkbug!"

B steadied her wobbling easel. "Watch where you're going!"

Jason snickered and dipped his brush in the orange paint. "Stinkbug!" he repeated to himself as if he was proud of his joke.

B fumed. She stared at Jason's paints. "S-P-I-L-L," she whispered under her breath.

Jason's easel pitched toward him. His paint tray flipped upside down, landing on his jeans before clattering to the floor.

Seeing Jason Jameson get what he deserves, B thought. *Now, that's a work of art!*

"Class, class!" Miss Willow cried over the chorus of laughter. "Back to your work, please!" She ran for the paper-towel dispenser.

Jason stared at the spatters of green, orange, red, and white paint that plastered his jeans so thickly you could barely see the blue cloth.

"You look like a Jackson Pollock painting," Kim said. "You know, the abstract spattery stuff?"

"Very funny," Jason snapped. He scrubbed at the paint with a paper towel, but that only smeared the splatters into a horrible mess.

"Run along to the washroom and get yourself cleaned up," Miss Willow said, handing Jason more towels and a hall pass. "You can go to the nurse's for a change of clothes."

B bit her lip and stared closely at her painting. Oh, she shouldn't have done that, she knew. But it had been worth it. She glanced sideways at Trina. The new girl seemed to be working hard not to laugh. B gave her a wink, and Trina nearly lost the battle.

With Jason gone, the atmosphere lifted. B decided to tackle Nightshade's whiskers again.

"I'm painting my cat, Nightshade," B told Trina in a low voice. "He's kind of like a miniature panther. I love black cats, and I especially love *the* Black Cats! Do you?"

Trina pursed her lips. "Umm . . . huh?"

B stopped in midstroke. "You know! The *Black Cats*? The band?"

Trina studied her shoes. "Never heard of them."

"Never heard of . . ." B checked her astonishment. She didn't want to embarrass her new friend. "Well, then," she said, "you're in for a treat. They're fantastic. My best friend, George, won two tickets to their concert Saturday, and he's taking me. I'm their biggest fan."

Trina, who had thus far painted only one black stroke on her sheet of paper, rinsed her brush rapidly in the cup of water B'd gotten her.

"What's the matter?" B asked.

"Can I get another sheet of paper?" Trina said. "I . . . I changed my mind. I don't want to do a panther. I think I'll do a penguin instead."

B shrugged. "Okay." She got Trina a fresh sheet, then tackled Nightshade's whiskers once more. They came out even better the second time. She was just finishing the last one when the bell rang.

"What's your next class?" B said, turning to Trina's easel. But her new classmate was already gone. B caught sight of her plaid backpack disappearing out the art room door. Too bad — B had planned to show her around the building a bit, maybe compare schedules. Even though Trina was definitely shy, B felt sure she was going to like this new girl.

There was no sign of Trina in second period, but in the hall on the way to English, B spotted Trina just as George came around a corner.

"Hey, Trina, meet George," B said. "He's the friend I was telling you about, remember? The concert tickets?"

Trina blinked, then nodded. She held out a hand for George to shake. So old-fashioned! But George took Trina's hand and shook it without any fuss.

"George, this is Trina Lang. She's new. We had art together."

George nodded. "Hey, Trina. Nice to meet you. What class do you have next?"

Trina consulted an index card. "Umm... English. Bishop. Room two-two-seven."

"That's where we're headed," B said. "C'mon. Mr. Bishop's great. You'll like him."

"Yeah, he can do magic," George said.

Trina paused. "Huh?"

B suppressed a smile. George was far more right than he knew! "He means," she told Trina, "that Mr. Bishop's great at doing magic tricks. You know, pull the rabbit out of the hat? That sort of thing."

"Oh." Trina headed down the hall, reading the numbers on each classroom door.

Mr. Bishop was more than just a great, if eccentric, English teacher. He held important duties at the Magical Rhyming Society, or M.R.S., where witches studied and practiced casting spells using rhymes. And he was B's magic tutor, assigned to help her figure out how her unusual brand of word-spelling magic worked, and, perhaps more important, how it didn't.

But Trina didn't need to know about any of that. If she ever found out . . . B shuddered. Trina *couldn't* know. No one was supposed to know that she and Mr. Bishop were witches — except George, who had accidentally discovered B's secret, and that couldn't happen again.

"Want some chocolate, Trina?" George said, holding out a bag of Enchanted Chocolate Peanut Butter Pillows.

"George never leaves home without chocolate," B observed as Trina helped herself to a handful. "That's why I keep him around."

"Enchanted Chocolate! That's my favorite kind," Trina said.

"Me, too." B didn't bother mentioning that her father worked for Enchanted Chocolates Worldwide. Some kids were jealous of B for that very reason — but it wasn't as if he brought home bags of chocolate every night. Once a week, maybe. What none of the other kids knew was that Enchanted Chocolates was a company run by witches.

They reached Mr. Bishop's classroom. Trina wiped chocolate from the corner of her mouth. B noticed George peering at Trina curiously.

"What's up, George?"

George's answer was directed at Trina, not B. "I could swear I've seen you somewhere before."

Trina gulped down a big chocolate mouthful and shook her head. "Doubt it," she said. "I just moved here from practically across the country."

The bell rang, and the students took their seats. As usual, Mr. Bishop was late to arrive. Trina slipped into the only empty seat left, against the wall near the sawdust-filled cage where Mozart, the class pet hamster, snoozed.

"Hey, look, everybody, Kat-trina the mouse is sitting next to the hamster," Jason Jameson said. "Rodent to rodent, how cozy."

"Knock it off, Jason," Jamal Burns said.

"Good morning, good morning, good morning," Mr. Bishop said, breezing through the doorway, dressed from head to toe in black, with a chain of Navajo turquoise beads at his throat. He twirled the tip of his dark beard between his thumb and fingertip, and clapped his hands. "Ah! She's here. You must be Katrina, yes? Our new student?"

Trina blinked and shrank back in her chair, but nodded.

"Stand up, stand up!" Mr. Bishop said, heading for her desk. "Tell us all about yourself."

B hunched down in her seat, embarrassed on Trina's behalf. She knew how much *she* hated being thrust into the spotlight like that, by teachers trying to be friendly. Poor Trina. She must have stage fright, too.

Trina stood up. Her fingers entwined behind her back, and she twisted awkwardly. "There's not much to tell."

"There's something special about everyone. Tell us one special thing about you." Mr. Bishop beamed at her expectantly.

"Honestly, there isn't," Trina said, her face flushing pink. She stared at the top of her desk. "I'm just an everyday student."

Mr. Bishop took a step back, hesitated, then turned toward the chalkboard. "Well, Katrina, we're delighted to have you here," he said. "Everyday students are welcome in my class every day."

Trina sat down, looking relieved.

"Today we're going to talk about poetry," Mr. Bishop said, taking his chalk in hand. "We have so much to learn, and there will be a flash quiz at the end of class. We'll discuss rhythm, meter, and rhyme; alliteration and assonance; form and genre. Everybody ready?" He whirled about and faced the class. B turned sideways to see her classmates' dumbstruck faces.

"What? You don't want a poetry test today?" Mr. Bishop teased. Twenty heads shook vehemently.

"Then how about we analyze an old-time poetry classic instead?"

The class sighed in relief.

Mr. Bishop produced a stack of papers. "Everybody take a copy of this handout and pass it back. We'll start with one of my all-time favorites: 'The Cremation of Sam McGee' by Robert Service. *There are strange things done in the midnight sun by the men who moil for gold. . . .*"

They took turns reading stanzas aloud. When the bell rang, B almost didn't hear it because the class was laughing so hard at Mr. Bishop's reenactment of the poem. She stuffed her things into her bag quickly and turned to leave with George and Trina.

"Can I see you for a minute, B?" Mr. Bishop said just as they reached the door.

"I'll see you at lunch," B told her friends.

The room emptied. "What's up, Mr. Bishop?" B asked. "Need to reschedule our next magic lesson?"

"Nope," her teacher said. "I got a note from Madame Mellifluous this morning. M.R.S. Express Post! A little slip of parchment appeared wrapped around my breakfast fork."

B laughed. That would be just Madame Mel's style. "What did the note say?" B asked.

"It said," Mr. Bishop replied, pulling a lavender slip from his pocket and unrolling it, "*'that the novice's preliminary oral progress assessment has been tentatively calendared for tomorrow afternoon pending confirmation by the addressee.'*"

B wiggled a finger in her ear. "Huh? Translation, please?"

Mr. Bishop handed her the slip. "It means that the novice — that's you, the beginner at magic — will meet with Madame Mel tomorrow afternoon for a preliminary oral progress assessment. In other words, a spoken test."

B's schoolbag thudded on the floor. "A magic test? *Tomorrow?*"

Chapter 2

Mr. Bishop sprinkled a handful of hamster chow in Mozart's food dish. "Yep. That's not a problem, is it?"

"You bet it's a problem!" B cried. "I'm not ready for a magic test. I'm terrible at spoken tests. I get so nervous. And everything I do with magic comes out screwy anyway."

Mr. Bishop raised a finger in front of his mouth. "Careful, B, that no one hears you," he said in a low voice. "Besides, that's nonsense. 'Everything' you do with magic does not come out wrong. You're incredibly talented."

B sank into a desk chair. "What am I going to

do? I'll fail — I know I will. And then what? Will they kick me out of magic tutoring?"

Mr. Bishop twirled the tip of his beard with one finger. "B, re-*lax*! It's only a very beginner test, basic spells and potions. It's as much a test of how well *I'm* teaching *you* as it is a measure of your ability."

"Sure," B said miserably. "I've heard that before."

"You'll be fine. Now, get to lunch, and enjoy the rest of your day. Piece of cake."

B stood and shuffled toward the door. "'Kay."

"And, B?"

She paused.

"I'm glad you and George have made friends with the new student. That's very thoughtful of you."

B nodded, then left the classroom. She tried, all the way to the cafeteria, to shake off the dread she felt about tomorrow's magic test. Would it be in front of a roomful of witches? The first time B went to the M.R.S., Madame Mel put her on the spot in front of hundreds of witches and asked B to perform a spell. B ended up shattering all the lamps in the room. Just the memory of it made her shudder.

She pushed the cafeteria door open and looked for George and Trina. She spotted them just as George tossed a grape high in the air and caught it in his mouth. She waved to them both, then hurried through the line to pick up her own tray. Tacos today, with peanut butter cookies for dessert. Definitely could be worse!

She sat down with her friends.

"Knock-knock," George said, looking at her and smiling expectantly.

B grinned at Trina. "Who's there?"

"Katrina."

The new girl's eyebrows rose.

"Katrina who?" B said obediently.

"Ka-Trina come out and play kickball?"

"George, that's awful!" B protested, but Trina's eyes sparkled.

"Ooh, here's another. Knock-knock," George said.

"Who's there?" B and Trina said in unison.

"Katrina."

"Katrina who?"

"Ka-Trina take my test for me today, teacher? I forgot to study."

Trina groaned, but she couldn't quite stop herself from laughing.

"George, you need to go to a joke doctor," B said. "I think your funny bone is sprained."

"I've got one," Trina said.

B stuffed a bite of taco in her mouth and turned to listen.

"Knock-knock," Trina said.

"Who's there?" B and George chimed.

"George-and-B."

"George-and-B who?"

"Georgian bee makes more honey than an Alabama bee!"

George gave Trina a high five. "Your jokes are even cheesier than mine."

"And that's saying something," B said, sticking a straw in her chocolate milk.

Trina smiled and tucked a flyaway strand of hair back into her unruly bun. Her cheeks shone pink from laughter. She looked very different from the shy girl B had met in art class just that morning.

"I'm so glad you moved here, Trina!" B exclaimed. "We're going to have a lot of fun."

The bell for fifth period rang. Trina stood up and wadded her lunch wrappers into a ball. "Thanks, B," she said. "I'm glad I met both of you. See you tomorrow." And she headed for the door.

"Tomorrow?" B asked George. "We might have more classes together later."

"Nope," George said, dumping his napkins into the trash and returning his tray. "I saw her schedule. She doesn't have any other classes with either of us."

"Too bad. She's fun."

George held the cafeteria door open for B. "Yeah. I think so, too." He fished into his pocket and pulled out his bag of Peanut Butter Pillows. "Must — have — chocolate. I'm starving!"

B poked his belly. "How can you be starving when you just had lunch?"

After school, B watched out for Trina along the hall of lockers, but there was no sign of her. She headed outside for the bus line, and then noticed Trina standing by herself, some distance away from the other kids, her plaid backpack dangling from one hand.

"Hey, Trina!" B called, jogging over to her.

"Incoming!" George hollered, sprinting toward them like he'd been shot from a cannon.

Trina nudged B with an elbow. "Does he always make an entrance like this?"

"Only outdoors," B said, rolling her eyes.

"Want us to walk you home?" George offered.

Trina took a step backward. "No, thanks. I, uh, I'm all set. I've got a . . . someone coming to pick me up. Any minute now. So thanks."

She kept her gaze pointed at the beginning of the drive leading up to the school. B paused curiously. Was it her imagination or was Trina acting strangely?

"Whaddya say, George? It's a nice afternoon," B said. "Want to ditch the bus and walk home with me?"

"Sure," George said. "Race you to the street." Before B could protest, George bolted down the sidewalk.

"See you, Trina," B said, and she took off, hoofing along after George. She didn't have butter's chance on hot toast of catching George, and she knew it. George was just enjoying his own speed.

A long, gleaming dark sedan pulled into the driveway just as B reached George, who had flopped down on the grass to wait for her. George whistled at the sight of the car as he stood up. "Lookit those wheels!" he said. "Practically a limo."

"Nah, it isn't really," B said. "Just a big car."

"Yeah, but what's it doing at school?"

"Search me." B hitched her backpack up higher. "Wait a minute." She shielded her eyes from the afternoon sunlight with her hand. "Look, George. Trina's getting into that car."

The sedan glided around the drop-off circle and headed back down the drive, toward where they stood openmouthed.

"Turn around," B whispered. "Keep walking. Don't let Trina see us staring at her car."

They turned abruptly and headed down the street toward home. The sedan turned onto the street and passed them, its engine barely making a sound.

"That car has a *professional* driver," George said. "A guy in a suit and one of those chauffeur hats."

"S'pose she's a princess?" B asked.

"Maybe she's in the Witness Protection Program, and that driver guy works for the government," George said. "I know! Maybe, *maybe* her father is a former member of the Mafia who got busted for money laundering, and only escaped jail time by testifying against the godfather! Maybe . . ."

B laughed. "I don't know, George," she said. "That's a lot of maybes."

"I know, but when have you ever seen a kid picked up from school by a chauffeur in a limo?"

B shook her head. "Never."

"Maybe it's not the Witness Protection Program," George conceded, "but it's a mystery, just the same."

"Think we can solve it?"

George grinned. "All it takes is a little magic."

Chapter 3

B stopped in her tracks and moaned. *"Magic!"*

George looked alarmed. "What's the matter?"

B walked in circles around her best friend. "I meant to tell you! I didn't have any warning, and there is no way I'm going to pass . . ."

"Pass what?"

B stopped pacing. "My first ever magic test. With Madame Mellifluous, the Grande Mistress of the Magical Rhyming Society."

George nodded. "Ah. Her."

Butterflies were having a heyday inside B's stomach, and the test was still twenty-four hours away. How horrible would she feel tomorrow?

"Will you help me study?"

"Sure. I'll try. But how can I? I don't know any-thing about it." A worried look crossed his face. He patted his forehead. "You're not going to practice on me, are you?"

B flinched, and shook her head. Last time she experimented with magic around George, he turned into a zebra, and it was a stressful week of trial and error before B figured out a reversal for the spell.

"I won't do any magic on you," B said. "Just help me think of ideas. Things I can practice."

He snapped his fingers. "Here's a practice spell for you. Conjure up some chocolate for me."

B looked carefully around. The street where they walked was quiet. No cars, no playing kids. There weren't even any houses close by. She nodded. It should be safe enough.

In an unmowed patch of grass between the side-walk and the road, a tall stand of late-autumn wildflowers bloomed. B picked two, one with deli-cate, white lacy blossoms, and the other with short, brick red blooms.

George looked puzzled. "What do I do with them?"

"Take a good look at them."

When George had had a chance to look, B took back the flowers, turned aside so she couldn't see George, and spelled "C-H-O-C-O-L-A-T-E."

"Unbelievable!" cried George, who'd been peeking over her shoulder. The delicate stems and flower petals transformed into wafer-thin filaments of creamy brown chocolate, still etched with all the lines and patterns they'd had as wildflowers. "I've never seen anything like it."

George took one of the flowers and bit off a blossom. He sighed with pleasure. "Awesome. Your dad's factory couldn't make it any better," he pronounced.

B grinned. Some of her worry lifted from her shoulders.

George fed the entire flower, long stem and all, into his mouth. "You've got nothing to worry about on that test." He devoured the other flower and licked his lips. "Just make this Madame Mel lady some chocolate and you'll definitely pass."

*   *   *

The next morning B's eyes flew open well before her alarm clock had a chance to make its bullfrog croak. Thoughts of her test filled her with dread. *Maybe,* she thought, *some extra practice before breakfast will do me good.*

B scanned the room for inspiration. She spotted her collection of stuffed animals piled under her Black Cats poster. She loved to hear the Black Cats sing. Maybe she could form her own band. "S-I-N-G," she instructed the colorful lump of toys.

Instead of a choir singing in harmony, her stuffed bear roared, her purple puppy yapped, the pink seal barked, the parrot squawked, and the huge bumblebee George had given her last Christmas buzzed like a chain saw. Nightshade leaped from beneath the pile. He arched his back, every hair standing to attention, hissed at the noisy animals, and darted from B's room.

"Sorry, Nightshade," B called. "S-I-L-E-N-C-E," she spelled quickly. The duck-billed platypus gave one final grunt before the room went quiet. Why couldn't her magic work the way she wanted it to? How was she ever going to pass her witchy test?

She stared at her Black Cats poster again. She knew what her problem was. She couldn't concentrate. Last night her older sister, Dawn, had been watching an entertainment news program on television, and the host had said the Black Cats would be making a special announcement the next morning about the remaining stops on their concert tour. B couldn't wait to hear it. New songs? New dance routines? Maybe some sort of contest, with winners from the audience.

B gave up magic practice and crawled out from under the covers. She jumped in the shower, dressed, and headed downstairs for breakfast.

Her mother was in the kitchen, sprinkling chopped macadamia nuts and lime juice over halved papayas filled with fresh pineapple. Hawaiian breakfast boats, she called them. A frying pan full of eggs was scrambling itself on the stove, the spatula stirring and flipping the eggs to perfection. B gave her mom a hug, then turned on the kitchen television.

"Set the table, will you, B?" her mother said.

B distributed the plates, then reached for a pile of napkins. She cleared her mind and focused on them. "F-O-L-D," she said. The napkins leaped into the air one by one and folded themselves — one became an airplane, another an origami swan. One became a Spanish galleon in full sail. B smiled as she admired her handiwork. *Maybe the test will go okay.*

"Lovely, B," her mom said, setting a platter of eggs on the table. "I think, though, that they may be hard to use. Why do you have the TV on?"

"There's supposed to be a . . . Here it is!" B pointed to the screen as the Black Cats' familiar logo flashed above the news reporter's shoulder.

"The Black Cats are still at the top of the charts, and their concert tour has been the most talked-about in years. But now, in a stunning turn of events, the Black Cats announced this morning that they're canceling the remainder of their sold-out, forty-seven-city worldwide tour."

The handful of forks B was holding clattered to the floor. "Noooooo!"

B's mom placed comforting hands on B's shoulders as the view on the television screen shifted from the newsroom to the steps of a hotel with palm trees in the distance. "Here's Len Michaels, the Black Cats' publicist, speaking from Los Angeles earlier this morning," the reporter's voice said. A man in a suit and sunglasses spoke into a cluster of microphones.

"The Black Cats regret to announce they are canceling the remainder of their Cats Unite tour and taking a break from recording for personal reasons. Ticket buyers will receive full refunds."

A reporter waved a notebook and called out, "Is it true that their last concert was cut short?"

The Black Cats' publicist raked his fingers through his short, slicked-back hair. "A sprinkler system malfunction. Yes, that's right. But it —"

The same reporter interrupted again, "Wasn't it during their 'Wet Cats' song?"

"The audience thought it was part of the performance, but that has nothing to do with this announcement," the publicist said, removing his sunglasses and rubbing his eyes before continuing. "The Black Cats want to thank their fans for their support and apologize again. I've got no further comment at this time."

The camera cut back to the newsroom. B's grip on the remote control shook as she clicked the television off.

"Oh, honey, I'm so sorry," her mom said, wrapping her arms around B. "And you had backstage passes."

B buried her face in her mom's fuzzy bathrobe. "I can't believe it."

She heard her dad and Dawn coming down the stairs, so she pulled herself together. She picked at her breakfast without eating much, then kissed her parents good-bye and ran for the bus stop, early for once. George was there waiting for her — that almost *never* happened — so B figured he'd heard the news as well. One look at his face confirmed it.

"Canceled!" George moaned when the bus arrived. "Why on earth would they cancel?"

"Why couldn't they have canceled the rest of their tour starting *next* week?" B said as they settled into a seat.

George shook his head. "For the biggest band around to suddenly break up . . . It's horrible!" He dropped his backpack underneath the seat. "I've been counting the days till the concert ever since I got the tickets."

B folded her arms across her chest and slumped low in her seat. Telephone poles whizzed past her view. "What a rotten way to start the day." Splatters of rain began to streak against the window. "And I've still got that test to worry about."

"Test?" George said. "Oh. Right. That one."

The bus slowed, and a group of kids boarded. One of the boys pointed out the window. "Look at that car," he said. George and B looked to see Trina's car pulling out from an intersection on its way to school.

George bent over low so he could speak in a quieter voice. "I've been thinking more about Trina," he said. "What if she's the daughter of an oil tycoon?"

B shrugged.

"Or maybe some software billionaire?"

"What if she is?" B said. "There must be a reason why she's keeping things from us. I think she wants to be friends."

"Well, whatever her story is, I think I can get it

out of her," George said, crossing his hands behind his head. "My special, never-fail method."

B prodded him in the ribs. "Which is?"

"Wait and see."

B's morning classes limped along miserably. In art, she smudged purple background paint all over Nightshade's paws. In history, she nearly blurted out "Potions!" when the answer should have been "Poland." And every kid she bumped into had the same thing on their minds — the canceled concert. She felt about as cheerful as an alligator on a diet when she slouched into her chair in English class.

"Morning, B." Trina's voice made B jump.

B tried to shake off her gloom. "Where were you this morning?" B asked. "You missed art class."

Trina shrugged her shoulders out of her plaid backpack. "Oh, I had some stuff I had to take care of. You know. From . . . moving here."

B nodded but she wasn't sure she believed her.

Trina sat down. "Hey, how come everybody looks so upset today?"

"Haven't you heard?" B said. "Of course, I forgot you're not into the Black Cats. They were going to have a concert here this weekend, and just this morning they canceled the rest of their tour."

Trina watched B thoughtfully. "I guess that must be really hard on a band's fans, huh?"

B rested her head on her folded arms. "I was so excited to go Saturday. It would have been my first ever rock concert."

Trina patted B's shoulder. "I'm sorry you're so disappointed, B. I really am."

"Thanks."

"Hey, Katrina, good morning!"

B blinked and raised her head off the desk. Something didn't seem right. Was that *Jason Jameson's* voice sounding polite and friendly?

If her ears were deceiving her, so were her eyes. It *was* Jason, and he had perched himself on Trina's desk. Trina looked like a caged animal, desperate for an escape.

"How're you settling into the new school?" Jason said. "Learning your way around okay?"

Trina nodded.

"Anything I can help you with? Did you have any trouble finding your way *home* yesterday?"

He'd seen Katrina's car and the driver, B realized, and was kissing up to her because he figured she was rich, as always, Jason's slimy motives were crystal clear, and B had no patience to spare for him. Not today.

"Jason Jameson, get *off* Trina's desk!" she said. "She sure doesn't want *you* there."

Jason sneered at her. "Buzz off, Bumble*bee*," he said. "I'm just having a chat with my new friend Katrina. Keep your nose out of other people's business."

Trina dropped a pencil on purpose, and Jason jumped down to grab it. She quickly dumped her books on her desk so that Jason couldn't sit there again. "To answer your question, Jason, I'm settling in just fine. My *friends*, B and George, have been showing me around. So, thanks for asking, but I'm all set."

Jason frowned, then quickly smiled again, showing his braces. "If you ever decide you want to hang out with nonlosers, let me know."

The bell rang, and George ran into the room, followed by Mr. Bishop. George scooted to his seat. He passed B a note, whispering, "For Trina."

B glanced at the note before passing it on. *"Hey, Trina,"* it read. *"How do you like your new school? Is it better or worse than your old one? — George."*

Mr. Bishop started bouncing around the front of the room talking about poetry. B slipped Trina the note and peered sideways at her. Trina bit her lower lip, then wrote something on the note and slipped it back to B.

"Hey, George," it read. *"Some parts are better, and some parts are worse. — Trina."*

B handed George the note, and it soon came back to her.

"Bet you're not used to this fall weather or all this rain."

B slid the note to Trina. It returned.

"I'm used to fall and rain. ☞"

George took another stab at his not-so-subtle game. B began to worry that Mr. Bishop was going to catch her passing notes.

"So, are they mostly Lakers fans in your neck of the woods? Nicks? Bulls? Celtics?"

Trina's reply: *"I don't know. I'm not really into football."*

B smothered a laugh. George was listing *basketball* teams in a desperate attempt to find out where Trina came from. She'd never heard of the Black Cats and didn't know one sport from another. *George's never-fail method is no match for Trina*, B decided.

George was furiously writing another note when Mr. Bishop's classroom phone buzzed. George hid his paper. Mr. Bishop answered the call, nodded, then hung up the receiver. "Katrina," he said, "you're needed down in the office. Some, er, old friends are eager to see you. You'd probably better take your bag. I'll have someone get the homework assignment to you, okay?"

Old friends? All these missed classes? What was going on?

Trina nodded and rose, gathering her things. She didn't look surprised or upset at all, even though

Jason Jameson made a little *oooh* sound. She turned to face him suddenly, and he sat up straight, as if it were someone else who'd done it.

Mr. Bishop wrapped up the poetry lesson by assigning a group project. "Pick a popular song," Mr. Bishop said. "Any song you like. Write down the lyrics and analyze their poetic elements. Then, using the tune from the song, write some lyrics of your own."

Jenny Springbranch's hand shot into the air. "Can we pick our own groups, Mr. Bishop?"

"Nope," Mr. Bishop said. "I'm assigning the groups."

"Mr. Bishop," Jason called out, "I'll be happy to take Katrina her assignment. Why don't you put her with me?"

Mr. Bishop's eyes sparkled under his thick, dark eyebrows. "That's very generous of you, Jason, but I've already assigned our newest student to George and B."

George and B exchanged excited glances. It sounded like a fun project. And maybe, in the process, they'd solve the mystery of Trina!

Chapter 4

"I've got an idea for how we can learn more about Trina," George told B as they left gym class two periods later. "Want to meet up right after school?"

"Can't," B said, feeling the lunar moths stirring up her stomach again. "I've got that test."

"Oh. Right." George gave B's shoulder a friendly punch. "What're you worried about? You'll be great!"

"Thanks," B said. "I'm not so sure."

George checked his watch. "So, you should be back from the ... whatchyoucallit ... by around four o'clock, right?"

"The M.R.S.," B said. "Yeah, I should back by then."

"Perfect. That's not too late. I'll meet you here by the front entrance."

B hoisted her backpack over her other shoulder. "What've you got in mind?"

"You just focus on your test," George said; then he disappeared down the hall to his next class.

Somehow B got through the rest of the school day. She shuffled through Mr. Bishop's classroom door five minutes after the last bell rang.

"There you are! Let's go; we can't keep Madame Mel waiting." He pulled the classroom door shut after first peering down the hall in both directions. "Get a good sleep last night? Eat a power breakfast? Ready for action?"

B set her backpack down next to Mozart's cage. "Let's get this over with."

Mr. Bishop's eyebrow rose but he ignored B's remark. Instead, he spoke a traveling spell.

"Wild winds that whistle from south, east,
and west,
Whisk us away to B's first magic test."

The familiar travel-spell cyclone whipped through their hair and transported them to the M.R.S.

They had landed in a hallway just outside a large circular door that was thickly studded with round medallions of purple, green, and blue glass, all inlaid in silver.

"Let me guess," B said, searching for a peephole. "Madame Mel's office."

"Naturally." Mr. Bishop pressed one of the medallions — B never would have guessed it was the doorbell. A dizzying peal of chimes rang out.

The door opened, and Madame Mel's head poked through. Her baby blue hair was tucked into a bun, as usual, but a large peacock feather poked out from the coil of hair. She peered at B through her purple spectacles, perched as always at the tip of her long thin nose.

"Come in, come in!" she cried. "You're twelve seconds late. What a day, what a fuss! I've misplaced my best pen, my Crystal Ballphone keeps dialing Madagascar, and my teakettle won't boil. It just blows soap bubbles. Silly witch practical jokes."

She beckoned them both inside. B gazed at Madame Mellifluous's office. Teetering towers of books lined the walls. Huge tapestry cushions were scattered across the carpet in front of the fire. An antique globe spun slowly, a model moon orbiting around it. Fluttering over Madame Mel's desk were a dozen butterflies. B looked closer. They were wafer-thin butterfly cookies, hovering over a plate. Madame Mel's empty teacup rattled indignantly in its saucer, but over in the corner, instead of boiling over its steady blue flame, the teakettle puffed out pink and purple bubbles faster than they could pop.

And sprawled on a chair, soaking in the sunlight that poured in from a round window, was a live skunk.

B took a step back.

"Oh, it's all right," Madame Mel said briskly, shuffling through a stack of parchments on her desk. "It's only Hermes. He won't spray you unless you annoy him. Which I surely hope you won't, because I've just had the carpet shampooed. Now, where on earth is that pen?"

"Madame Mel?" B ventured.

"Hm?"

"I think it's on your head."

The Grande Mistress paused, groped at her hair, then plucked out the feather stuck into her blue bun. "So it is." She nodded at B, and gave Mr. Bishop a wink. "Your student knows what to do with her eyes, it appears. Let's see if she knows what to do with her magic."

B gulped.

"Good luck, B," Mr. Bishop called on his way out. "Just relax. You'll be fine."

Easy for you to say, B thought.

Madame Mel seated herself behind her desk. With a swoosh of her sparkling sleeve, she swept all the parchments onto the floor and sent the butterfly cookies flapping over to the window. Then she snapped her fingers at the skunk. "Hermes! I need you, please."

The skunk slowly roused itself, slid off the chair, and waddled over to Madame Mel. She scooped him up and set him on the desk, where he proceeded to sniff for butterfly cookie crumbs.

"Now, B, let me explain the testing procedure. There will be three tasks. First, a basic spell. Second, a potion. And third, an object transformation spell. Got that?"

B nodded, her mind racing. That wasn't much detail to go on.

"Would you begin by making Hermes talk?"

B relaxed. "Sure. That's an easy one. I've made Mr. Bishop's hamster, Mozart, speak lots of times." She cleared her mind of distractions, focused on the foraging skunk, and said, "S-P-E-A-K."

Hermes peered at B. He blinked, stretched, yawned, then curled himself into a ball for another rest.

Uh-oh. It hadn't worked!

"S-P-E-A-K," she whispered, repeating the spell as softly as possible, just in case.

"Was there a topic," Hermes's voice said, sounding thin and refined, "upon which you wished me to converse?" He shut his eyes as though he were drifting back to sleep.

B sagged with relief. "Anything you like," she said.

"Somnology interests me," Hermes said.

"Som-*what*?"

"Somnology. The scientific study of sleep." Hermes shifted his position to find a more comfortable curve for his body. He let out a long, slow breath. "Sleep is underappreciated. Lack of sleep" — he stretched his spine once more — "is associated with a wide range of health problems, in humans as well as skunks. Sleep can be divided into four stages . . ."

B glanced at Madame Mel to see how she was reacting to B's performance thus far. Her chin rested in her hand, her elbow propped on her desk, and her eyelids, behind her spectacles, were drooping.

". . . with most dreaming taking place during the rapid-eye-movement stage. . . ."

B coughed loudly. Madame Mel's eyes flew open. "Hm? Oh. Sorry about that. Hermes's lectures always make me sleepy."

"Where has he learned so much?" B asked. "He sounds like a science teacher!"

"Reading, of course," Madame Mel said. "The same way science teachers and anybody else learns. You read the paper for me, don't you, Hermes?"

Hermes sniffed. "When I must. I much prefer the *Journal of Magical Medicine*."

"Who doesn't?" Madame Mel said dryly. "Give me an article on sleep science over the funny pages any day. Turn him off for me, will you, B?"

"S-P-E-E-C-H-L-E-S-S." Hermes's mouth went silent. He nuzzled deeper into the folds of Madame Mel's sleeves, till only his face, with its blinking button eyes, poked out.

"Thank you. Nicely done."

B blushed with pleasure. She'd done it. Her first test had obviously gone well. "I like Hermes," B said, grinning with relief. "I get along well with small mammals."

"That will be useful, I'm sure. Now, let's move along, shall we?" Madame Mel pulled a drawer right out of the desk and dumped out its contents. A crazy jumble of odd bits and bric-a-brac spilled out onto the desk. B scanned the assortment. Her palms began to sweat.

Madame Mel set a cauldron on her desk. "Please select from these items, B, anything you wish, and use them to make a potion."

B swallowed and stared at the assortment of ingredients. Her mind was as empty as Madame Mel's desk had been a minute before.

"Whenever you're ready. I'm waiting."

Chapter 5

"What kind of potion?" B was pretty sure Madame Mel could tell she was stalling.

"I leave it to your creativity."

Relax, B. You can do this. You've done potions before. B took a deep breath. Odd bits of leather, string, ribbon, crystals, pencils, markers, coins, ornaments, earrings, amulets, spices, snacks, arrowheads, nuts and bolts, pebbles, feathers, twigs, tools . . . There was neither rhyme nor reason to the collection of junk from Madame Mel's drawer. Lots to work with, but nothing that suggested a theme. It was just a mess.

She thought of what she knew about potions.

The real trick wasn't so much in the ingredients. It was in your state of mind as you chose them.

She riffled through the junk heap. A huge, hairy spider made her jump. She poked it. Only rubber, but her skin still tingled, giving her an idea.

B reached for the cauldron. She dropped in the rubber spider, an orange feather, and a can of soda. Madame Mel's eyes followed B's movements. B tried to ignore it. She reached for a pepper grinder and cranked a few twists into the pot.

Close. One more thing. But what?

She plucked a short strand of miniature Christmas lights from the debris and stuffed it into the cauldron. She closed her eyes to concentrate on the ingredients and how they made her feel. Tickle her skin, tickle her tongue, tickle her nose, tickle her fancy! She chuckled to herself.

"T-I-C-K-L-E," she said. The ingredients spun and melded into a shimmery pink sauce. Whew! B poured some into a tiny goblet and held it up in the air.

"Shall I drink it?" she asked Madame Mel.

"Let me." The Grande Mistress of the Magical Rhyming Society tossed back the tickle potion in one quick gulp. For a moment she sat quietly, her face still with concentration. A nostril twitched, and then the other.

"*Hoo-hah-hah-hah-hooooo! Hee hee!*"

Hermes took a flying leap off Madame Mel's lap and scuttled underneath a grandfather clock.

"*Hah! HAH! Ooh, oh, make it stop, ah-hah-hah-hah-hoo!*"

Madame Mel threw herself back in her rocking chair, clutching at her sides. The chair went over backward. All B could see were Madame Mel's electric blue boots kicking furiously in midair. Then there was silence.

"Madame Mel! Are you okay?" B ran around the desk, afraid to find her injured from her fall. But Madame Mel was only gasping for breath so she could laugh harder. She slid out of her upturned chair, still writhing with laughter.

"Make . . . *hee!* . . . it . . . *hoo-hoo-heh* . . . stop!"

"I don't know how to make it stop," B said. "Do you?"

"Can't . . . *heh-heh-heh* . . . rhyme . . . *hah-hah* . . . like this!"

What could she spell? UNFUNNY? SERIOUS? What if Madame Mel ended up in the hospital because of B's renegade potions?

At last Madame Mel's hysterical laughter subsided. She lay on the floor for a few seconds, limp and exhausted, before climbing up and brushing herself off.

"Sorry about that," B said. "It did tickle you, though, didn't it?"

Madame Mel adjusted her powder blue bun and peered down her nose at B. "Hmph."

Uh-oh.

After setting her chair back on its legs, Madame Mel sat down once more and folded her hands together. "For the final part of your exam, please turn my paperweight into an orange."

B turned to see a glass paperweight, etched to look like a basketball, holding down a stack of parchment.

"A basketball?" B said, turning it over in her hands.

"I'm especially fond of college hoops," Madame Mel said. "Turn it into an orange, please."

Just yesterday she had turned flowers into chocolate. She could do this. She thought about the paperweight and thought about oranges. Basketball made her think of George. Her best friend. George loved chocolate. *Focus, B!* Paperweight. Orange. "O-R-A-N-G-E," she spelled.

The glass basketball turned into an orange . . . made out of chocolate.

"Look," B said, her heart sinking. "I can peel off the dark chocolate skin. Ohh, it's milk chocolate inside. That's pretty neat, huh?"

Madame Mel held out her hand. B handed her the half-peeled orange.

"Look at the texture," B added, feeling like a television salesman. "It's so lifelike."

Madame Mel finished peeling the "orange" and popped a section into her mouth.

"Lovely chocolate," she said, licking her fingers. "As good as Enchanted Chocolates."

B reached for her last straw. "Any chance it's orange flavored?"

Madame Mel didn't answer. "Excuse me for a moment." She pressed a button on her desk, and in seconds the door opened. Mr. Bishop entered. B wandered over to where Hermes sat, sunning himself in front of the grandfather clock, while Madame Mel and Mr. Bishop whispered to each other.

"S-P-E-A-K," B whispered. "How'd I do, Hermes?"

"A conundrum," the skunk replied. "Is a laugh a tickle?"

"I didn't mean to."

"And that orange that wasn't an orange . . . even if she liked the chocolate."

B heard the door close. She turned and saw that Madame Mel had left the room.

"Sorry, pal," B whispered. "S-P-E-E-C-H-L-E-S-S." She turned to where her magic tutor stood, his hands clasped behind his back.

Mr. Bishop sighed and shook his head. "I'm sorry. I'm afraid you didn't pass. Don't feel bad. Many witches don't pass their first test on the first try. If anything, the fault is mine. I was eager for Madame Mel to see the progress you were making."

B flopped into Hermes's old chair. "I'm sorry I made you look bad."

Mr. Bishop shook his head. "It's nothing. No harm is done. You can retake the test."

B felt like her face had been splashed with cold water. "You mean I have to do this again?"

"Don't worry. You'll be fine. Let's get back to school."

B barely listened to his traveling couplet. First she lost the Black Cats concert; then she failed her magic test. What else could go wrong today? In seconds she was standing in Mr. Bishop's English classroom. She grabbed her bag, said good-bye to her teacher and to Mozart, and hurried down the hall toward the front entrance. It was almost 4:00.

George stood waiting for her, munching from a big bag of Enchanted Chocolate Double-Dipped Pretzels. "How'd it go?"

B didn't respond.

"Need a pretzel?"

B took a handful.

"I'm sorry, B. Shake it off, you know? There's always next time."

"Ugh! Next time."

"Forget about next time," George said, quickly changing course. "Listen, I've been thinking about the Trina thing. I've got a special, surefire, one hundred percent guaranteed way to find out her secret. We need to figure out where she lives."

"Why?"

"We've got to take her the English homework assignment."

"How can we figure that out?" B asked. "Calling Information?"

"Already tried that. Nope, my way is more sophisticated. Pure genius. Watch and weep." He pushed open the swinging door that led to the school's main office.

Most of the staff people had left for the day, except for Mrs. Armstrong, the secretary, who, B sometimes thought, really ran the school, not the principal.

"How're you doing, Mrs. A?" George said,

leaning against the counter and flashing his biggest smile.

"Fine, thanks, George," Mrs. Armstrong replied. "Just got these report card grades to verify in the computer before I can leave for the day."

"Grades good this term?" George asked casually.

Mrs. Armstrong wagged a finger at him. "Mind your business, young man." Then she smiled. "Yours are good. As always."

"Excellent." He set his bag of chocolate pretzels on the counter as though he wasn't giving a bit of thought to what he did. B noticed Mrs. Armstrong's eyes jump to the silver-and-purple bag, then back again to her stack of report cards.

"Like chocolate, Mrs. A?"

"Oh . . . I shouldn't." She patted her belly.

"D'you like chocolate *pretzels*? Just try one of these. They're amazing!" George waved the bag under her nose.

Mrs. Armstrong hesitated, then plunged her hand in. At the first taste, she closed her eyes and sighed. George sneaked a grin at B.

"Something I can help you two with?" Mrs. Armstrong said, reaching once more for the pretzels.

"Oh. Yeah," George said as though he'd almost forgotten. "We've got a homework assignment we need to deliver. To Katrina Lang, the new girl in our class? She's been assigned to be in our group for a poetry project."

"How nice," Mrs. Armstrong said, turning her focus to her computer.

"But we don't know where she lives," George said, pouring a few more chocolate pretzels onto the counter. "Would you mind looking it up for us?"

Mrs. Armstrong hesitated.

"It's a big project. We need to start right away, or our grades might suffer," George said.

Mrs. Armstrong popped one more pretzel in her mouth, then scooched her chair back. "Oh, okay. For you, George." She left the room, and George gave B a quick high five. In no time Mrs. Armstrong returned with an index card in her hand.

"I've copied down her address," she said. "It's very thoughtful of you to take the assignment to her."

"Oh, it's nothing," George said. "Here. Take the last two pretzels."

Once outside, George consulted the card. "Forty-seven Blossom Lane." He whistled. "Isn't that where they have the big gates up around all the mansions?"

"Figures," B said. "If she's got a chauffeur, she's probably got a nice house, too." She tugged on George's backpack. "Come on, let's go. We'll get there quicker if we cut through the woods behind the soccer fields."

They reached Blossom Lane and began searching for house numbers.

"What's that one?"

"I can't tell," B said. "The house is so far back I can't see the number."

"Anything on the mailbox?"

B checked. "No mailbox at all. Maybe the mailman brings their mail straight to the swimming pool."

"Maybe the butler takes the helicopter into town to pick it —"

"Look!" B interrupted. "That house is number thirty-nine."

"Forty-one, forty-three, forty-five," George counted. He pointed to a tall house of dark redbrick, with a pointy tower and a fountain in the yard. The driveway was buzzing with people and cars, as if they were having a party. "That must be Trina's house."

B hurried forward for a closer look. "Are you sure? Sometimes house numbers don't work like they're supposed to."

George gestured toward a black sedan sweeping through the electronic gates and into the curving driveway. "The car would be one giveaway. And there's Trina." His face fell. "She saw us."

"Some spies we are," B said. "Now we look like snoops. No better than Jason Jameson."

"Nah," George said. "C'mon, let's go. Don't be embarrassed. We're here for a good reason. The homework project, remember?"

"Suppose she invites us in? Man, I'd love to see the inside of that place."

George elbowed B. Then B saw why.

"Hey, guys." It was Trina, approaching them across the perfectly trimmed lawns. "What are you doing here?" She looked nervous, glancing over her shoulder at the cars and people.

Was she mad? Hard to tell.

"Homework," George said. "Mr. Bishop assigned you to our group for a poetry project. Sounds pretty big, so, we, er . . ."

"We got your address from the office and stopped by to drop it off," B finished. "Mr. Bishop wants us to pick a favorite song, analyze the poetic elements in the lyrics, then write new lyrics. Want to, maybe, start working on it a little today?" B watched for Trina's reaction. "Since, you know, we're here and everything?"

"It sounds like fun," Trina said. "But now's not a good time."

"Ka-tri-na!" A voice from the direction of the house made Trina jump. It was shrill, and a little crackly.

"I've got to go," Trina said. "Sorry we can't get started now. That's my grandmother. I need to practice . . . We need to work on a . . . project. Inside. An indoor project. We've got company."

"A *practicing* project?" B asked, puzzled.

"One that can't wait," Trina continued. "So, tomorrow, okay? Gotta go now. Bye!"

And she turned and ran across the lawns. George and B watched her disappear into the huge front doorway of the home. Then they both turned to leave.

"Practicing," George mused. "I know! Maybe she's a Ninjitsu black belt, doing her daily exercises. Spies do martial arts all the time." He dropped his body low into a karatelike crouch, bracing his arms against an imaginary attacker. "Though it seems strange to think she'd practice on her old granny. . . ."

"Spies use weapons now," B said. "She's probably got to practice detonating the grenade secretly hidden in her lip gloss case."

"I hope she doesn't practice that on her granny, either."

B laughed. "She's probably just a princess, practicing shaking hands with dictators. Or maybe she's just a shy girl with a crabby grandmother. Let's go home."

Chapter 6

B decided that she would wear a Black Cats shirt every day that week as a symbol of mourning for the broken band. At school, she found she wasn't the only one clad in Black Cats wear. She counted eight Black Cats hooded sweatshirts, six T-shirts, and three hats, all with sparkly Black Cats logos. She spotted Trina easily, as she was one of her only friends not wearing any Black Cats memorabilia. B waved but Trina didn't seem to notice.

"Hi, Trina!" B called but when Trina walked by, B noticed the headphones tucked into each ear. Trina was singing along quietly and enjoying herself. B decided not to disturb her.

B took a final gulp of pomegranate juice just as Jamal Burns slammed his locker, turned, and ran right into her. Dark red juice spilled all over her Black Cats shirt.

"Aargh!" Cold juice ran down her front, staining the light gray fabric. "That'll never wash out!"

"Oops. Sorry," Jamal said, disappearing into his homeroom.

The bell rang, and the hall emptied quickly as students scurried away. B stared at the hideous stain on her shirt. The Black Cats logo showed three black cats arching their backs and strutting underneath a full moon, but the pale gray moon was now maroon.

B looked around. Nobody in sight. Staring at the stained Blacks Cats logo, B whispered, "C-L-E-A-N." The juice leaped out of the fibers of her sweatshirt in a big, jiggly pomegranate blob, then evaporated. Her shirt looked fresh as new.

"Holy cats," B whispered, grinning. Sometimes she even impressed herself.

Just then, she heard a sound she'd never heard in school before. *A meow?*

From around the corner came a small kitten,

smoky black from head to tail. The kitten scampered toward her and rubbed against her legs, then jumped into her arms.

B was stunned. How did a cat get here? She swallowed hard. Could she have accidentally conjured it up when she did her cleaning spell? It would be just the kind of thing her spells sometimes did. *Maybe*, B thought, *it was because I was looking at the Black Cats symbol when I made the spell.*

Now what? She was already late for class, but she couldn't go to class with a kitten. *Mrs. Armstrong will know what to do*, B thought.

B started carrying the kitten toward the office, when, with a meow, it faded and disappeared in her arms, leaving only a sparkle before it winked out.

No question — that cat was magical.

B stood still, thinking. One problem solved: no cat to explain away. Another problem discovered: B's crazy unpredictable magic was up to its usual tricks, and this time those tricks were creating living creatures! Good thing her favorite band wasn't the Mighty Mighty Mammoths.

"Do you guys want to come over today after school to start our poetry project?"

B, George, and Trina swiveled around in their seats. The bell had just rung to end English class.

"Yeah, I guess we could do that," George said to Trina, pretending to be nonchalant.

B tried not to smile. "We'd love to."

Jason leaned in closer. Eavesdropping, undoubtedly. That snoopy Jason Jameson!

"Why don't you meet me out front after school," suggested Trina, "and I can give you a ride?"

Interesting, thought B. *Why so open and inviting today, when yesterday she was so secretive?*

George sat up straighter in his chair. "Sure! Yeah. Absolutely. I love cars."

"Was there something you wanted to ask us, Jason?" B said.

"I've got nothing to ask you, *Wasp,* except for maybe when you're going to buzz away and never come back," Jason said. "I had a question for *Trina.* So, Trina, um, want me to come over some time and bring my Black Cats CDs? I remember you said you weren't familiar with them." He patted his chest. "I'm a Black Cats expert."

"Is that so?" Trina polished her glasses on her sweater, then peered at Jason. "I have a question for *you*. Why would you think I'd want to hang out with you, when you're always so rude to my friends?" She slung her plaid backpack over her shoulder. "C'mon, guys, let's go to lunch."

After school, George and B waited with Trina for her car to arrive.

"Have you guys got a favorite song you'd like to work on?" Trina began. "There's this new band I like called the Frog Princes, and I thought maybe . . ."

"Ssh!" B interrupted her. "Don't turn around, anyone. Trina, Jason Jameson is actually *hiding in the bushes* to spy on you."

"*What?*" Trina rolled her eyes in disgust. "What is the matter with that kid? Everywhere I go, he's in my face."

"Maybe he's got a crush on you," George said.

"Oh, good, here comes Rick," Trina said, visibly relieved. The long black sedan swept around the drive and into the parking lot.

"Rick?" B asked.

"The driver," Trina explained.

"Don't drool on the bushes, Jason," George called. His cover blown, Jason poked his face out of the shrubs to scowl at them.

They climbed into the backseat of the car, and Trina introduced them both to Rick, a short, muscular man with friendly eyes. "Afternoon, ladies and gentleman," he said, nodding to George. "Where are we bound today?"

"Just home, thanks," Trina said. B elbowed George so he'd stop *ooh*ing and ogling the car's luxurious leather interior and all its features: a minirefrigerator, snack bar, television, and even a video game system.

"Wow, do you use all this stuff?" George asked.

"Mostly only on long trips," Trina said. "Anyway, about the song for our project, what would you think of —"

"Where d'you *get* a car like this?" George burst out.

B watched Trina's face closely. George was excited about the car, she knew, but she could tell he was also keeping up his quest to find out where Trina came from.

"At a dealership, I guess," Trina said. "I didn't buy it personally."

Rick pulled the car into the driveway at Trina's house. They climbed out, and Trina invited them inside through the back door. They passed through the kitchen, where Trina opened the fridge and offered them sodas and juice, then headed into the living room. It was big, but otherwise pretty much like any normal living room, except that the walls were bare. No, not bare exactly — nails were spaced high on the wall as if they once held pictures. B noticed a bunch of picture frames leaning against the wall near the bookcase, with the pictures themselves facing the wall.

"You just moved in, right?" B said. "You're unpacked except for the pictures."

"Oh, you don't want to see those," Trina said quickly. "They're . . . boring. I have an uncle who likes to photograph . . . dirt. Grandma says we have to hang them on the walls, but I don't want to." Trina grabbed a throw off the couch and tossed it over the stack of frames. "Pull up a chair, guys, and make yourselves at home."

"Hey, is that an actual suit of armor?" George headed toward the front entryway, where a knight stood guarding the door.

"Wait! You can't go out in the hall." Trina blushed as they both turned to look at her. "You, um, have to stay in here. My grandma doesn't really like visitors, so I'm only allowed to have people in the kitchen and the living room. The noise in the hallway would disturb her."

B and George sat back down. B felt bad for Trina, living with a grandma who seemed so restrictive. Still, why all these secrets? Yesterday they weren't welcome inside. Today they could come in, but so many things were off-limits. Strange.

"What about your parents?" George said. "Do they like visitors?"

"I live with my grandma," Trina said. "My parents are, um, traveling."

A telephone rang in the kitchen, and Trina excused herself to go answer it. While she was away, George and B exchanged a look. They didn't need to speak. B knew George was thinking the same thing she was. Trina was getting more mysterious by the minute.

Chapter 7

"I'm back," Trina said, returning to the living room. "Let's get started. Did you guys have a song in mind?"

"'Yowl'!" George and B said the word together.

"What's that?" Trina said. Then, as her gaze rested on B's Black Cats sweatshirt, she snapped her fingers. "I know. It's by that band everyone's talking about, right?"

"The Black Cats!" B exclaimed. "You still haven't heard their music?"

Trina shrugged. "Maybe once or twice."

"I know," George said. "For our group project, instead of doing an essay or a poster, why don't we *sing* the new song we write? I'll bet Mr. Bishop would give extra credit for that."

"No way," B said. "You know I don't like performing in public."

"I don't sing."

George and B both looked at Trina. "Not even in the shower?" B asked.

"At *all*."

Even stage-fright B was surprised at the determination in Trina's voice.

"Okay," George said. "I guess we'll scrap that idea. The first thing we need to do is write down the lyrics to the song."

"Ready," B said, pulling out her notebook. "The song begins, 'Midnight in the alley, the cats are on the prowl, they see the full moon risin' —'"

George cut in. "'That's when they YOWL, yowl, yowl, yowl. . . .'"

"It's really just one 'Yowl.' The rest are the backup singers," B said.

"Doesn't matter," George replied. "It's still repetition. That's a poetic element."

"Whatever," B said, writing as fast as her hand would go. "'That's when they yowl, yowl, yowl, yowl, yowl. . . . That's when they yowl, yowl, yowl. . . .' Man, this line repeats three times! They could have thought up some lyrics with more variety."

"I thought you really liked the song," Trina said.

"Oh, definitely," B said. "I just don't like transcribing it."

George continued. "So after the third 'yowl, yowl, yowl' bit, they say, 'Throw your head back and HOWL, howl, howl, howl. . . .'"

"'The cats are on the prowl. *Yeah!*'" B finished her notes.

They wrote out the second verse in the same way, and once again it ended with plenty of yowls.

"No shortage of rhyme here," George said. "What about the next verse?"

"This one has a different meter. Slower," B said. "'Night's — the — hour — for — keep — ing — se — crets. . . .'"

"Is that the chorus?" George asked.

"The bridge," Trina said quickly.

B turned toward her, surprised. "The *who*?"

"The bridge," Trina said. "That's what you call that part of the song, where the verses and the tune change to something different. It's not the chorus; it's the bridge." She looked confused for a minute. "At least, I'm pretty sure I saw that once on a TV show."

"Learn something every day," George said. Then he burst into song. "'But — we — Black — Cats — ain't — got — se — crets,   want — the — whole — wide — world — to — hear — us — YOWL,   yowl, yowl, yowl!'"

"You were a little bit off there, George," B said. "It's 'But — we — Cats — ain't — got — no — se — crets. . . .'"

George shook his head. "No, I'm positive it's 'we Black Cats ain't got.'"

"Nope. They don't say 'Black' in that line," B said. "I've only listened to this song about a million times."

Trina cleared her throat. "You're both wrong. It's But — us — Cats — don't — want — no — se — crets."

George and B stared at Trina. "You said you didn't know the song!" B exclaimed.

"Who cares? I think she's right." George started singing again, and B joined in. Even Trina hummed along.

"Mad dogs in the alley
Show their teeth and growl.
But they're no match for street cats
Who bare their claws and YOWL, yowl, yowl,
    yowl. . . ."

B stopped singing. Even just humming, Trina's voice was amazing! It seemed to fill the room, despite the noise she and George made.

Trina swayed back and forth to the rhythm of the song, closed her eyes, and sang.

"Night's the hour for keeping secrets.
But us Cats don't want no secrets,
Want the whole wide world to hear us
    YOWL. . . ."

A trunk in the corner of the room sprang open with a bang all by itself, as if by magic. Clothes, shoes, and papers came flying out. Trina stopped singing. George shot a glance at B. She knew what he was thinking, because she had the same concern. She hadn't spelled a thing! How could her magic be this uncontrollable? What if Trina got suspicious?

Trina hurried to clean up the spilled things and close the trunk. "Boy, that's weird," she said anxiously. "Must be the springs are broken or something."

B wiped her sweaty palms on her jeans. Then she caught sight of something on the floor.

"That's a Black Cats suit!" B cried. "The catsuits they wear, with the rhinestones. And the boots! Where'd you get a costume like that?"

Trina didn't answer, but stuffed the costume back in the trunk and closed the lid.

"And where'd you learn to sing like that?" George demanded. "You said you *don't* sing, and you *don't* like the Black Cats! You . . . you could practically impersonate them."

Trina turned to face them, looking sheepish. "Well . . . ," she said, ". . . I guess I am a secret fan after all."

"Why keep it a secret?" B reached down and picked up a Black Cats album cover that had blown out of the trunk with the clothes, but escaped

Trina's notice. B stared at the cover. Then she stared back at Trina. She couldn't believe her eyes. Why hadn't she seen it before?

"Holy cats! *You're* the lead singer! You're KAT!"

Trina blew out a long, slow breath. "Well," she said, "so much for secrets. That one didn't even last a week."

George and B both sank down onto the couch, too stunned to speak. B pinched herself to make sure she wasn't dreaming.

"I knew I'd seen you before," George said. "I thought, maybe, I'd seen you at the mall." He laughed. "I guess I probably have seen you at the mall, at the record store."

"And the movies," B added. "Remember they did that movie last summer?"

Trina sat on the floor and plucked at the carpet.

"What's the matter, Trina?" George said, playing on an imaginary electric guitar. "I'd love to be in a rock band. Most kids would kill to be you."

"It is fun," Trina said. "But that's just the problem. Kids might think they'd like to be me, but once they find out I'm Kat from the Black Cats, they treat me differently. All they see is a rock singer." She leaned back on a cushion. "Not a person."

"Yeah, but . . ." George was so excited he could barely find the words. "You get to ride around in a limo, and travel all over the world, and . . . sign autographs!" He collapsed back into the couch. "Buckets of money for all the chocolate you could ever want!"

Trina laughed, but only for a second. "That stuff's fine, but people chasing you gets old pretty quick. Photographers and reporters'll follow you into the bathroom if they can."

B whistled. She'd never thought of it that way before.

"It's like hundreds of Jason Jamesons," Trina continued. "He's only hovering around because he thinks I'm rich. That's nothing compared to how people react when they find out you're *famous*." She sighed. "I thought, if I came here and lived with my grandma, I could start fresh." She smiled sadly. "It was really fun having genuine friends again."

B jumped up. "Well, who says we're going to change? We're not!"

"We're not like that," George said. "We were just surprised for a second. Nothing's going to be different."

Trina sat up. "You mean that?"

"Of course we do." B tossed a couch cushion at Trina playfully. "We can keep a secret, can't we, George?"

"Sure." George gave B a knowing look. She knew he was thinking of the secret they already shared — B's magic.

"We won't treat you differently, so long as you promise not to treat me differently when I'm a world-famous soccer player," George said.

They all laughed.

"Deal," Trina said. "What will you be famous for, B?"

B shrugged. "Oh, I dunno . . . I'm pretty good at, um, spelling."

Trina's eyes lit up. She lobbed the couch cushion back at B. "I get it — Spelling B! You'll be a world-famous spelling bee champion. You've got the perfect name for it."

B grimaced. "I don't need to be famous. I'd hate to have everyone watch me." B remembered her most recent spelling bee, before she understood how her spelling magic worked. She'd flooded the whole school building! "Let's get back to work on our project before it gets too late."

Trina jumped up. "I've got a better idea. You'll like this." She reopened the trunk in the corner. "Do you guys want to see my Black Cats stuff?"

"Absolutely!"

Trina unloaded one thing after another — costumes, props, promotional posters, jam session tapes, autographed photos. In no time the living room was full of Cat-abilia.

"This is so cool," George said. "You guys are the hottest band around. Why did you cancel your concert tour?"

Trina sank back on her heels. "I know. I'm so sad about it. I'll miss the band so much. They came over yesterday to say good-bye. At least for now." She pressed her lips together. "But, that's a band secret that I can't share." She shook her head. "Sorry."

B considered teasing her for more info, but the look on Trina's face changed her mind. She and George had almost stumbled onto the Black Cats' farewell yesterday. She tried not to show it, but she was even more impressed with Trina. It took the sting out of the canceled tour.

"We all felt terrible about it, but it was unavoidable."

"Ka-TRI-na!"

It was the crackly voice B'd heard the day before, calling from upstairs.

"Grandma," Trina said. "Sorry guys, but . . ."

"Are those children still here, Katrina?"

George and B climbed to their feet. "We were just leaving," B said. "We'll figure out another time to work on our project. Thanks for having us over, Trina."

"Yeah, and thanks for showing us all this stuff!" George said.

"Wow, can you believe that? Kat from the Black Cats, right in our class!" George exclaimed on the way home. "This kind of thing just doesn't *happen*!"

"I know," B said. "I'm so glad we got to know her first." B still had a strange feeling that there was something else Trina wasn't telling them.

George said, "So now I've got a witch and a Black Cat for a friend. Which reminds me . . . why did you use magic to open that trunk? That was pretty risky to do in front of somebody else, wasn't it?"

B shivered. "Oh, my gosh, I was so nervous that Trina would get suspicious. Turns out she was more worried about her own secret. But that's just it. I didn't *mean* to do it. I have no idea how it happened."

George scratched his curly blond head. "You mean, you didn't spell any words in your head or something?"

"I'm sure I didn't." B jumped over a puddle in the sidewalk. "Did I?"

George stopped to look at B. "You wouldn't ever let her in on the secret, would you?"

B shook her head. "No way. I can't. You're not even supposed to know, George. But I'm worried. There's more than just that trunk. Somehow, today, without meaning to, I conjured up a magical kitten. Something's really wrong. More proof that my magic is out of control."

Chapter 8

B arrived at school early the next day. She'd barely slept, worrying about her unpredictable magic, so in the morning she decided to go straight to the person who could help.

She tiptoed into Mr. Bishop's classroom. "Good morning."

Her magic tutor jumped at the sound of her voice. "B! What brings you here so early?"

B greeted Mozart and poured some kibbles into his dish. "It's my magic. It's gone haywire. First I failed the test. Then, yesterday morning, I did a quick spell to remove a stain from my shirt, and a little magical kitten appeared. I have no idea why. It jumped into my arms, then vanished."

"Hmm." Mr. Bishop twirled the tip of his black beard. "Go on."

"Then, yesterday afternoon, I was at a friend's house. I didn't spell anything. All of a sudden this trunk springs open, bang!" She closed Mozart's cage. "What's wrong with me?"

Mr. Bishop pulled on his jacket. "Hmm . . . could be a magical malady. And now's not a good time for one! Madame Mel asked to reschedule your makeup test for after school today. So we'd better get your magic examined."

"How?" Then B shook herself. "Wait a minute. Did you say my retest is *today*?"

Mr. Bishop nodded. "Same time, same place."

B rocked on the heels of her sneakers. "But I can't! I'm not ready. I need more time to iron out the kinks. And the kinks are getting weirder than ever."

"Then there's not a moment to lose." He looked at his watch. "Come on. I'll take you to someone who can help."

"Who?"

Mr. Bishop's cowboy boot heels clicked on the

floor as he moved to stand next to B. "To a witch doctor, of course!"

Mr. Bishop's travel spell deposited them in a waiting room filled with magical mobiles that spun without any breeze and chairs spangled with stars. In one corner sat a miserable-looking young witch with a boxful of tissues. Every time she coughed, a ladybug flew out from her throat.

"At least it's not spiders, Maudie," the older witch beside her said.

A witch in long, loose robes covered with cartoony pictures of frogs and a stethoscope around her neck handed them a clipboard.

"New patient? Yes, I thought so. Fill out these forms, please. All twenty-seven of them."

"Can we bypass the formalities this time, Dorcas?" Mr. Bishop said in a low voice. "This is a special, rush-rush case. This young lady here has a magical exam in just a few hours." He dropped his voice even lower. "I think she might have caught Spontaneous Spellulitis."

B gulped. That sounded awful!

The nurse's eyebrows rose. She consulted her watch, then beckoned for them to follow her. "Right this way."

She showed them into a small room with a counter, sink, desk, and cot. The walls were plastered with bits of parchment with poems written on them — things like, ORAL HYGIENE WON'T BE RUSHED, HAPPY TEETH ARE FLOSSED AND BRUSHED, and COLDS DON'T HAVE TO BE AN ISSUE, CATCH YOUR SNEEZES WITH A TISSUE.

"I thought you said this doctor treated magical maladies," B said, pointing to the couplets on the wall.

"Witches can get regular sicknesses, too," Mr. Bishop explained. "Dr. Jellicoe treats magical and nonmagical illness."

B was just reading the diploma on the wall for Marcellus K. Jellicoe, Doctor of Magical Medicine, when there was a knock at the door. "Who's there?" Mr. Bishop called.

"Doctor Boo," the voice replied.

"Doctor Boo who?" Mr. Bishop said, grinning at B.

The door burst open. "Don't cry — you're not getting shots today!" The doctor threw back his head and laughed. "That's a good one, isn't it? Just thought it up on my way down the hall."

B stared at the man. He was short, barely taller than B herself, and round as a soccer ball, yet light on his feet. His witching robe was a large white lab coat, big enough to fit around his girth. He thrust out a hand to B. "I'm Dr. Jellicoe. What can I do for you?"

"This is my student, B," Mr. Bishop said. "She's been having strange magical anomalies — spells cast around her when she never said a thing. She's a spelling witch, Doc, not a rhyming one. We wondered if you could give her a quick checkup before she goes into a witching exam today to make sure she doesn't have Spontaneous Spellulitis."

Dr. Jellicoe nodded. "I love a good case of Spellulitis! One time a patient of mine conjured a hot air balloon right in the middle of a shopping mall. Spellulitis is always good for some laughs."

"Not if it exposes witchcraft to the nonmagical world," Mr. Bishop said sternly.

Dr. Jellicoe sighed. "Yes, there is that aspect." He gestured for B to sit on the cot. He took a peculiar helmet out of a cupboard and put it on. Strange wires, visors, and antennae stuck out every which way. A rotating hourglass, a spinning prism, and a tuning fork all whizzed and spun.

"What's that thing for?" B asked.

"Protection," the doctor said. "If you've got runaway magic, anything might happen to me!" He snapped a purple visor over his eyes, then held up a magnifier flashlight to B's face. "Say 'ahhh.'"

B said, "Ahhh." Dr. Jellicoe peered into her throat.

"Excellent. Now, would you light my flashlight here for me?"

B spelled, "L-I-G-H-T," and a soft light beamed from his magnifier.

"Marvelous! Spelling magic." Dr. Jellicoe pulled four crazy-colored dice from his coat pocket, showed them to B, then shook them together between his cupped hands. "Think you can pull off a twenty-one for me?"

"Huh? Oh!" She quickly spelled the number, "T-W-E-N-T-Y O-N-E!"

The doctor tossed the dice onto the examining room counter. They rolled to a quick stop, a four, two sixes, and a five.

"Good . . . good." He pulled a little device from his pocket, made of a shiny rod around which rainbow-colored beads spun in circles, with no sign of attaching strings. Dr. Jellicoe studied the revolving beads and nodded. "Excellent. Your magical potency index is quite strong. Four point nine. Now, would you please conjure up some sort of dessert?"

"What kind?"

"Surprise me."

B thought for a minute. "S-U-N-D-A-E," she spelled. A jar on the counter became a goblet, piled high with ice cream, caramel sauce, and whipped cream.

Dr. Jellicoe licked his lips. He examined the sundae closely, then pulled a test tube from his pocket. He spooned ice cream into it and pulled a cord that dangled from the ceiling. A bell rang.

"Lab work!" he cried. A witch nurse in pale green scrub robes appeared and snatched away the tube. Once she'd shut the door, Dr. Jellicoe scooped a big mouthful right out of the sundae with his spoon.

"Nothing wrong with this magic," he said. "I don't even need to wait for lab results to know that." He took off his helmet. "You're fit as a frog, Miss B," he said. "Get hopping."

"Then what about all the odd things that keep happening around me?"

Dr. Jellicoe ate an even bigger spoonful of ice cream. "The world is nothing but a jumble of strange things happening everywhere you look. Some are magical; some are just part of being alive. But rest assured, your magic is in tip-top condition."

B wasn't convinced, but Mr. Bishop seemed entirely satisfied.

Dr. Jellicoe took a notepad and a pen from his pocket. "I have a prescription for you.

To make most magical malaises stop,
I prescribe one lollipop."

Dr. Jellicoe twirled his hand with a flourish, seemingly plucking a pink-striped sucker right out of thin air. He handed it to B.

B examined it. "Is this full of some magical medicine?" she asked. "Will it taste terrible?"

Dr. Jellicoe beamed at her. "Try it and see." B took a lick. Watermelon!

"Watermelon lollipops always make me feel better," Dr. Jellicoe said. He tucked his prescription pad back in his pocket. "You'll do fine in your magical exam today," he said. "Stay healthy!"

Mr. Bishop and B said good-bye and returned to the waiting room, where Mr. Bishop spoke a quick "back-to-school" couplet. They landed in Mr. Bishop's classroom just as the line of school buses began forming outside.

"I'd better get to homeroom," B said.

"Meet me here right after school, okay, B?"

B felt the lunar moths in her belly wake up from their sleep. Dr. Jellicoe may have said she was healthy, but right now B felt sick with worry.

Chapter 9

"Today, students, we will continue our work on animal portraits in a new medium — scratchboard. Instead of painting with dark strokes on white paper, we'll be etching white into black-coated paper. You need to suddenly see things in reverse. Let me demonstrate."

Miss Willow, immersed in her art lesson at the front of the room, was unaware of Jason harassing Trina behind the back row of easels.

"You're hiding something, Katrina. I know it."

Trina stared at the front of the room as if Miss Willow's demonstration contained the answer to the mysteries of the universe.

"Leave her *alone*," B said. "I'm sick of you bugging her."

"You're the only one who's bugging, Bumblebee," Jason replied.

"Why don't you make like a bee and buzz off?" B said a little too loudly.

"Beatrix," Miss Willow called, "please don't distract the class with your chatter."

B's cheeks burned. Jason hid behind his easel so Miss Willow wouldn't see him laughing.

Later that morning, on her way to English class, B saw Trina and waved to her. Then she paused. Following Trina a few yards back, cloak-and-dagger style, was Jason Jameson. He lurked in doorways and peered around corners, dodging other students while never losing sight of her.

"Jason's stalking Trina," B whispered to George as she caught up with him in the hall. "We've got to do something. He might stumble onto her secret."

Trina was walking toward them. She kept looking over her shoulder, but Jason would duck out of sight at the last minute.

"I know, but what?" George asked. "He's just curious, like we were."

"I know." B shook her head. "I still feel bad about the way we found out where she lives."

"Hi, B! Hi, George!" Trina said, looping arms with her two new friends and tugging them forward. "Have you spotted my shadow?" she whispered.

"Yeah, Jason's a real pest," B said, whipping her head around in time to catch Jason and glare at him.

"He won't leave me alone," Trina said, her shoulders sagging. "If he finds out, well, then I don't know what I'll do. I don't want to move again."

"Why don't we meet after school and work on our poetry project?" B asked, trying to cheer up Trina.

"I'm in!" George said.

"How can we with Mr. Nosy tagging along?" Trina asked sadly. "He'll ruin everything."

B pulled her friends to a stop outside their English classroom. "We'll think of something."

Mr. Bishop stepped into the hallway and said,

"Why don't you all come inside? Class is about to start. And that means you, too, Mr. Jameson."

Jason blushed as he slipped from behind the trophy case where he had been hiding and slinked, head down, into class.

B sat through the poetry lecture and readings, fuming over Jason Jameson's outrageous snooping. A pest like him was sure to turn up something sooner or later. Once he caught onto the fact that Trina was really Kat, the lead singer of the Black Cats, the whole town would know. Reporters and photographers would swarm all over Trina.... She'd probably have to move again! B glanced over at her new friend, who was busily taking notes on Mr. Bishop's lecture. *All she wants is to be normal,* B realized. *I've got to think of a way to get Jason Jameson off her back at least for a little while.*

Then she got an idea.

"Psst." George glanced over at her.

"Pssst." Trina looked up.

"Meet me at my locker after school," B breathed, barely doing more than mouthing the words. George and Trina nodded.

George and Trina were waiting for B when she reached her locker after the last period. It had taken her a minute to find Kim Silsby and her attached-at-the-hip best friend, Drake, and a minute more to persuade them to loan her their matching Black Cats sweatshirts, but they did.

"We can throw Jason off the scent with a little switcheroo," B said. "Here's the plan. . . ." She explained her idea.

Trina grinned. "That's perfect. I think it'll work."

"Incoming," George said, nodding toward the end of the corridor. "Jason's on his way."

"Make sure he sees us," B said. She and Trina stood back from the locker so all the world could see them slip on the matching black hooded sweatshirts. Then they took off down the crowded hall, side by side. B glanced back just enough to see Jason set off after them.

"Now," she whispered.

B and Trina began weaving in and out of their classmates, crossing paths again and again to confuse Jason as to which girl was which.

"Ready?" Trina whispered.

"Let's do it." B and Trina pulled up their hoods and parted ways, each one heading toward the other one's locker. When she passed a long, glassed-in trophy case, B glanced sideways and saw Jason's reflection following her. *Yes!* She hurried to Trina's locker. After pausing there for just a minute, she headed down the long corridor toward the cafeteria and picked up the pace, sensing Jason's impatience. If she could make it as far as the cafeteria, she should buy Trina enough time to sneak away to the library and meet George like they had planned.

Just then she felt a tap on the shoulder. "Hey, Trina," Jason said in a singsong voice. B turned around slowly to see Jason's face harden into a scowl of anger.

"Hello, Jason," she said in her sweetest voice. "Is there something I can help you with?"

"What in the heck do you think you're . . . Hey!"

B and Jason noticed Trina in the distance at the same time, wearing her Black Cats hoodie. Why was Trina still here, and not on her way home?

Why would she come back in the building, after all their efforts to double-switch Jason?

Jason took off after Trina, and B took off after him. Trina was booking it down the hall. B would never have guessed Trina could move so quickly. Jason was only barely keeping up. The hallways were nearly empty now, so B risked using some magic to slow Jason down. She hoped it wouldn't go haywire again.

"S-T-I-C-K-Y," she spelled, concentrating on Jason's shoes. His footfalls began to squeak; then each foot became stuck to the ground. Jason yelped in surprise as he struggled to wrench each sneaker off the floor, as if he'd stepped in a huge fresh wad of chewing gum. B giggled. This was a little too much fun.

Trina was opening the double doors to the gym when Jason recovered and took off after her, B right at his heels. Jason reached for Trina's hood and yanked it to reveal not Trina's long dark hair, but a mop of dirty blond curls.

George! B was so shocked, she nearly fell over.

"Why, you . . ." Jason fumed, kicking at a stray basketball.

George smiled and flashed B the thumbs-up. That was the signal: Trina had gotten away.

Trina greeted B and George with high fives all around — after she had checked to make sure B and George didn't have a Jason Jameson–size shadow. "We did it! Your plan was brilliant, B."

"Your and George's switch was what really did the trick," B said.

"I've got an idea — let's create a song inspired by Jason Jameson," George said, and then he began to sing off-key: *"When Jason comes a-stalking, we don't even care."*

"Keep going," B cheered.

"Oh, I'm horrible at rhyming. What rhymes with 'care'?" George asked.

B thought for a second and then dashed off all the rhyming words she could think of. "Bear. Dare. Fair. Hair. Pear."

Trina broke out into a silly grin and sang:

"When Jason comes a-stalking, we don't
even care.

He's no match for us; black cats are everywhere!"

Trina stopped singing abruptly and clasped both hands over her mouth.

"What is it, Trina?" George said. "Is Jason back?"

Trina shook her head vigorously and slowly lowered her hands. "I really shouldn't have done that."

"What?" B said, but then she looked around. She couldn't believe what she was seeing. She turned in a slow circle.

Black cats were everywhere. Crawling on bookshelves and lounging on tables. Swinging from light fixtures. The floor was covered in a sea of black cats. B had never seen so many felines in her life. "Holy cats!" she exclaimed.

Only one thing could cause this type of disaster — magic!

"Oh my gosh, oh my gosh, oh my gosh!" Trina's panic-stricken voice roused B from her own shock.

While Trina rushed around the library trying to herd the cats, George leaned in and whispered to B, "She's a witch, isn't she?" He sounded dazed, like someone waking from a dream. "One of the rhyming ones."

"No time for that now," B said. "We've got to help her." Now all B's recent magical problems — the trunk springing open, the mysterious black cat in the school — made sense. Her magic wasn't out of control; Trina's was.

B walked over to where Trina had stopped, holding two squirming cats. "It's all right, Trina," she said. The two cats wriggled free and B put her arm around her friend's shoulders. "It's all right. Or at least it will be."

"No, it isn't," Trina said, pulling away. "You don't understand."

"Yes," B said, "I do understand. Boy, do I understand. You're a witch."

Trina's eyes widened in shock.

"It's okay. I'm a witch, too."

For a second, B thought Trina might faint. The lead singer of the Black Cats blinked.

"My magic isn't always in control, either," B said.

George walked over, trying not to step on any cats. "What are we going to do about all these cats?"

"It's okay," B said to Trina. "He's not a witch, but he totally gets it."

"Maybe not totally . . . ," George mumbled.

"But I thought humans weren't ever supposed to know about the existence of witches. How does he know?" Trina looked from B to George.

"That's a long story." B stared at the hundreds of cats crawling around the library. "I think we should figure out how to fix this problem first."

Chapter 10

"Why don't you do another poem thingy to make the cats disappear?" George suggested.

"I don't know," Trina said, scooping up a cat that was rubbing up against her legs. "Usually one of the other Black Cats or my grandma has helped me undo any magical mistakes."

"So all the Black Cats are witches?" B asked. "And your grandma, too?"

Trina nodded. "Maybe the cats will just vanish in a minute."

"We can't risk it," B said. "What if one of the teachers decides to go to the library, or some kid wants to return a book after sports practice?"

"Or what if the cats find a way out?" George added, watching the creatures explore every inch of the library. "Cats are pretty smart, you know."

"I've never messed up this bad before," Trina said, as if she wasn't really listening.

"You can do it, Trina. Just relax and concentrate. You're great at rhyming." B tried to sound encouraging, but she knew Trina had to fix this. If someone stopped by the library, how would they ever explain?

Trina closed her eyes. She took a deep, singer's breath from her diaphragm, filling her body with air, then sang:

*"Cats, cats everywhere, from up high to way
    down low.
You all are black and beautiful, but now it's
    time go."*

And in a flash, the library was cat-free.

"Did it work?" Trina asked, her eyes still closed.

"See for yourself," B said.

Trina opened one eye, then the other, and let out a huge sigh of relief.

"That was crazy," George said, looking around to make sure every cat was gone.

Trina laughed a little, then turned to B. "Are you really a witch? I can't believe it!"

"Really and truly," B said. "But my magic is different from most witches'. I do spells by spelling words, not by speaking couplets. I'm still trying to get the hang of it."

"Wow, I never heard of spelling magic." Trina looked at B more closely. "My magic's offbeat, too. Speaking spells doesn't work for me. I've got to sing them."

"A singing witch!" B smiled. "And that fits, since you're such an incredible singer anyway." Then B snapped her fingers. "That's it!"

Trina nodded.

"*What's* it?" George asked.

"The reason the Black Cats broke up. I get it! You can't have a singing witch singing all those songs. It would turn the world upside down."

Trina sighed. "Pretty much. I caused a lot of havoc before we figured it out. I moved out here to live with my grandma. She's a singing witch like me. She's trying to help me control my powers, but it's not easy."

"I know what you mean," B said. "Maybe in the M.R.S. library there's a book that explains what to do about that. If there was a way you could sing with the band again, would you want to?"

"More than anything," Trina said. "I miss it so much. I feel like a fish out of water without my singing."

"Wow," George said. "I can't believe it. Both my friends have these amazing superpowers, and what've I got? A decent soccer scoring average. Big deal."

"It *is* a big deal," B said. "You're going to be a soccer star someday! That's a superpower. And believe me, magic isn't everything. Sometimes it's more trouble than it's worth. You've seen it yourself."

B knew that George remembered some of B's magical mishaps, yet he still didn't seem convinced.

"Friendship matters more than magic," Trina said, looking at them both seriously. "You're a terrific friend, George. Both of you are. I'm really lucky to have met you." She smiled. "Thanks for your help with the Jason switcheroo after school, too."

B dropped her backpack on the ground. "After school," she repeated. "*Right* after school. Oh, no!"

Her magic test! She'd forgotten all about it! B scooped up her bag, turned around, and started running.

"Wait up!" George was chasing her.

"What's the matter?" Trina was following, too.

B's feet tore up the sidewalk. What should she tell them? She didn't want Trina to know that she was such a witching disaster that she needed a remedial makeup magic test.

"I, uh, have a tutoring appointment with a teacher after school," B managed to gasp between sprinting strides. "Forgot about it. Hope I'm not too late! See you tomorrow."

B vaulted up the school stairs in one giant step, wrenched the door open, and skidded through the freshly waxed corridors.

"Watch where you're going," the janitor hollered after her.

She threw open the door to Mr. Bishop's room. He was at his desk reading a book. He closed the pages with a thud.

"I'm sorry!" she blurted out. "I had a friend emergency, and I just . . ."

B's voice trailed off when she saw the look on Mr. Bishop's face.

"Keeping Madame Mel waiting is generally not the wisest idea," he said. "I called and postponed your test after you didn't show up."

B's knees wobbled. She slid into a chair. Saved! "Thanks."

"If we leave right now, we'll just make your new appointment." He reached for B's arm, uttered a couplet, and in seconds the traveling spell deposited them once more in the corridor outside Madame Mel's curious door. Her head poked out before they could even knock.

"Hurry in, hurry in!" Madame Mel intoned. "Heavens, how I hate to be kept waiting!" She seemed annoyed, but not really cross. B still couldn't believe her good luck. She hoped it would hold long enough for her to pass the test.

B followed the Grande Mistress of the M.R.S. into her office, spotted Hermes on the carpet, and quickly began the first spell. "S-P-E-A-K —"

"Ah, hold it there a minute." Madame Mel cut her off. "Each test is different. Can't have you knowing the questions in advance, can we?"

"That wouldn't do at all," chipped in Hermes. B smiled to herself. Her spell might not count, but at least it had worked!

"Indeed," Madame Mel continued. "So this time, make Hermes fly, if you'd be so kind."

B studied Hermes's bulgy-looking body. He looked as aviation-worthy as a serving of mashed potatoes.

"Okay, Hermes, don't be scared. F-L-Y."

Hermes lolled over onto his back, poking his little paws up in the air, and basked in the sunshine. Not flying at all. B felt her palms begin to sweat.

"Maybe he needs help with takeoff," she told Madame Mel, stalling for time and praying her theory was right. She reached down and picked up Hermes, depositing him gently on Madame Mel's desk, noting with surprise how silky-soft his fur felt.

"Hermes, run across the desk and leap into the air, okay?"

"As you suggest. Please be prepared to catch me if your magic is, ahem, insufficient." Hermes waddled at full tilt across the end of the desk, then leaped into the air. B held her breath.

He dipped down only slightly. Then he spread out all four paws and glided leisurely around the room, soaring above both their heads.

"This is rather exhilarating, I must say!" he called with a high-pitched giggle. "Look at me! Wheeeeeee!"

B watched Madame Mel's face anxiously. The corners of the Grande Mistress's mouth twitched as Hermes's fur ruffled in the breeze. "He's starting to show off," Madame Mel observed.

"Better come down now," B told the skunk.

"Certainly not! This is the best flying spell I've had in years!"

"Never mind; let him enjoy himself," Madame Mel said. "I'll tend to him later. Now, for the potion. This time, I will choose the type of brew."

B's hopes fell. She'd been planning to concoct a truth potion, something she'd had some success with in the past.

Madame Mel dumped out the drawer of ingredients once more. "Would you make a politeness potion?"

After some consideration, she chose a glove, a breath mint, a moist towelette, and a postage stamp — which made her think of sending thank-you notes. She wasn't sure if it was a strong enough mixture of politeness objects, but she closed her eyes, took a deep breath, and spelled, "P-O-L-I-T-E."

B opened her eyes and saw that the objects had formed into a tangerine-colored liquid. She breathed its citrusy fragrance before pouring it into a little goblet. Her nose tingled. Uh-oh . . . she'd inhaled some of the potion!

Madame Mel pursed her lips and drank a sip.

"Thank you, B," she said, her voice syrupy-sweet. "I don't know when I've tasted a lovelier potion."

"No, thank *you*," B replied. "It was a charming idea for an assignment."

"My pleasure entirely," Madame Mel said. "Won't you pull up a chair? Please, make yourself at home. Can I offer you any refreshment? It's nearly teatime."

"Oh, I'd hate to trouble you," B said. "I'm perfectly all right. But thanks for offering."

Madame Mel hiccupped. "Gracious! Excuse me." She dabbed at the corner of her lips with a napkin. "I do believe your potion has been successful, B."

"He flies through the air with the greatest of ease . . . ," warbled Hermes, floating belly up and pretending to backstroke. His altitude was dropping. B plucked him from midair before he bumped into the grandfather clock.

"I say!" the skunk cried indignantly. "Another flying spell, please!"

"S-P-E-E-C-H-L-E-S-S," B spelled before he could lecture her any further. Then she returned to her chair.

"Awfully kind of you to rescue my skunk. And my clock," Madame Mel said.

"Not at all," B said. "My pleasure."

"Ahem. Yes, well, I do apologize for asking anything more of you, B, but we must be moving on with the test. I have another student waiting, and I'd hate to inconvenience him. If you'd be so kind, for your final exercise, would you turn this globe" — she gestured to the magnificent antique globe of the world behind her desk — "into cheese?"

"What an interesting challenge," B said. "I'd be honored to give it a try." *Holy cats!* B thought. *This politeness potion is a doozy! I can't get it out of my head.*

She focused on the spinning model of the world and thought about cheese. Cheese, cheese, a world of cheese. She thought of the magic-run creamery her mother frequented, the Magical Moo, and all the delicious cheeses they sold from around the world. Swiss, Camembert, Manchego, Stilton, American, Cheddar, provolone . . .

This was it. Would she pass the test? Were her other spells enough?

"C-H-E-E-S-E."

Madame Mel gasped with delight. She opened a cupboard and pulled out a tray covered with assorted crackers.

"What a masterpiece!" she exclaimed. "Parmesan for Italy, all the little Swiss cheese holes in the Alps." She dipped a cracker into the Pacific Ocean and tasted it. *"Mmm . . .* you have an artist's touch. Not many students would have thought to make a blue cheese dip for the oceans."

B dipped a cracker into the British Isles and tasted the soft, nutty Cheddar.

Madame Mel clapped both her hands, and the door to her office opened. Mr. Bishop appeared, smiling. "Bravo," Madame Mel said. "Your pupil did a marvelous job today. She passes the test with flying colors."

"And flying skunks," B said.

"Now, then, B." Madame Mel slipped Hermes a cracker, then put the tray away. "You've earned a reward for your performance today. You may conjure it up yourself. Would you spell 'CHARM,' please? And concentrate on the experience of taking this test. "

"C-H-A-R-M," B said as soon as she felt ready. She held out her wrist, where she always wore the silver charm bracelet she'd received when she first figured out her powers. A new charm appeared next to the sparkling silver "B." It was a smiling skunk nibbling a wedge of cheese.

B showed it to Hermes. "Now I'll never forget you, Hermes," she said. He nuzzled her hand in reply.

"Lovely to visit with you two, but I must get on to my next appointment," Madame Mel said. "Whew! That politeness potion is only just beginning to clear up. Strong stuff, B. Excellent work. See you soon!"

Chapter 11

Back in Mr. Bishop's classroom and with the test behind her, B still couldn't relax. She remembered the other events of the day — especially the surprise news about Trina's magic, and how it put an end to the Black Cats. There must be some way to help her out.

"You've tutored other beginner witches besides me, haven't you, Mr. Bishop?"

Her teacher nodded. "Many of them. Why do you ask?"

Should she divulge the secret? If it could bring Trina some help . . .

"You know Katrina, the new student, right?" B paused. "She's a, well, did you know —"

"She's a witch," Mr. Bishop interrupted. "She's got a special brand of magic, just like you."

B's eyes widened. "You knew? Why didn't you tell me?"

"It was her secret to tell," Mr. Bishop said, taking a seat on his desk.

"Then you know about her problem?" B began to pace from Mozart's cage to Mr. Bishop's desk and back again. Should she reveal the secret about the Black Cats, too? "Well, um, Trina's sad about the singing thing, because . . . she really loves to sing, and she's great at it, only since that's how her magic works, she doesn't dare. It'd be kind of like me competing in spelling bees. Not the best idea."

Mr. Bishop opened a desk drawer and began searching for something. "You wouldn't, by any chance, have a particular reason for being interested in this dilemma, would you?" He grinned. "A reason that has something to do with that sweatshirt you have on?"

B stopped pacing for a second and looked down at her borrowed band sweatshirt. "Is there anything you can do to help?"

Mr. Bishop leaned back in his chair and laughed. "I know all about Trina. And about the Black Cats." He pulled a parcel from his pocket and unwrapped the tissue paper wrapping. "I've been working on something to help her. This is an amulet to block her magic if she wears it when she sings." He held up a necklace with a silver pendant shaped like a treble clef. "I've been having a bit of trouble making it work. Amulets are a tricky business. Maybe you can help."

"Me?" How could she help? She was good at making messes, not cleaning them up.

"Yes — you know Trina and the Black Cats better than I do." Mr. Bishop began to swing the amulet back and forth. "We can make it your next lesson. Complex spells."

"What?" She'd just passed her first M.R.S. exam. She wasn't sure she was ready for anything complex.

"Some magic requires a series of spells. I've prepared the amulet to provide lasting protective powers, but I need someone to cast the spells specific to Trina." He handed the necklace to B. "I know you can do it. Take your time."

B stared at the amulet and thought about Trina, her voice, and all of the Black Cats songs B loved. She imagined the concert and how badly she'd wanted to go.

"S-I-N-G-I-N-G," B began. The treble clef pendant rotated in midair on its silver chain. "S-P-E-L-L C-A-S-T-I-N-G." A ripple of rainbow prism color flashed across its surface. "S-H-I-E-L-D." B finished her triple-spell incantation, and the silver amulet glowed with silver-white light.

"Singing. Spell casting. Shield," Mr. Bishop repeated. "It could work!"

"Do you think so?" B asked, trying not to smile too widely.

"Strong desire makes strong magic," Mr. Bishop said. "There's only one way to find out. Why don't you present this to Trina yourself?"

The next morning, B and George cornered Trina by her locker. B looked both ways to make sure no one was close by to hear. "I've got something for you," she said.

Trina opened the package and pulled out the necklace and pendant. "Wow, thanks! That's so pretty. You didn't have to do that." Trina fastened it around her neck, obviously pleased.

"It's not just a necklace," B said. "It's an amulet to shield your singing magic. If you wear this when you sing, you won't create crazy spells."

Trina's eyes were wide. She fingered the treble clef. "*You* made this?"

B blushed. "Well, I did have some help from a friend." She grinned. "I am your biggest fan, you know."

"Watch it, there," George said. "I think *I* am."

Trina's eyes shone. "Is it really true? Can I sing again?"

"Try it and see," B said.

"What, here? In school?"

"Trust me," B said, crossing her fingers and toes and holding her breath. It had to work. It just had to.

Trina bit her lip. "Okay. Here's what I'll do. I'll

sing the first song that ever produced a spell for me. It was at my cousin's birthday party just a few days after my eleventh birthday." She pointed to George.

"*Happy birthday to you! Happy birthday to you! You look like a monkey, and you smell like one, too!*"

George sniffed his underarms. Trina and B leaned in and sniffed, too.

Trina laughed delightedly. "You're fine. I don't even want to tell you what happened to my cousin Andrew."

They all laughed. Trina flung out her arms and spun around. "I can't believe it! I can sing again!" She stopped and grinned at her friends. "I've got to go call my manager right away. The concert tour is back on!" She ran off.

"Holy cats!" B whooped.

"What's the matter, B?" Kim Silsby said, pausing on her way down the hall.

"The Black Cats are back!" B cried. "The Black Cats are BACK!"

*   *   *

"George, have you ever heard so much noise in your entire life?" B yelled.

"What?"

"I said, 'Have you ever heard so much noise in your entire life?'"

"What?"

"Never mind!" Even screaming, she couldn't make George hear her.

It was Saturday night. They had pushed their way through the throngs of screaming Black Cats fans that filled the stadium, heading for their front-row seats. The opening band was finishing its act, but the fifteen thousand people gathered to see the Black Cats were too excited to pay much attention to them.

"Hey, this is us," George said. "Front and center!" He bounced up and down in the springy seats. "Can you believe it? Front row at the Black Cats, all for winning a spelling bee?"

"You were the winner, not me," B reminded him.

"Yeah, well, you would have won if it weren't for your magic," George said. He dug in his pocket. "Backstage passes, too!"

B nodded. She scanned the crowd behind them. The stadium was full now, and the crowd had begun chanting, "Black! Cats! Black! Cats!"

"How much longer until they start?" B asked. George peered at his watch.

Just then the lights went out. For a second the arena fell almost silent. Then strobe lights began to flash. The audience whistled and stomped their feet. A massive spotlight swirled around on the back curtain, way up toward the ceiling.

Loud guitar chords ripped through the massive speakers. Everyone screamed. Drums kicked in, and everyone went wild.

Then, from high above the stage, a giant crescent moon suspended by cables appeared in the spotlight, with girls in black perching on its inner curve, and Trina on the very tip.

"Kat! Kat! Kat!" screamed the fans.

"Trina! Trina!" George and B added. She looked so different in her cat costume and makeup.

The moon descended slowly. The band members swayed to the beat.

"Look at her up there! Can you believe it?"

George said, elbowing B. "Does it seem possible that that's our poetry project partner?"

"Not really," B said, laughing.

When the moon was about three feet off the ground, it halted. Kat, dressed in a black catsuit studded with rhinestones, leaped off the platform, landing in a catlike crouch.

"Midnight in the alley," she sang. *"The cats are on the prowl, they see the full moon risin'...."*

Just then a pair of security guards in black clothes appeared in front of George and B. "This way, please," one of them said.

"What's the matter?" said George, panicked.

"Just follow us, please," one security guard shouted over the music.

B's pulse pounded in her ears, louder even than the bass drum. She hurried after the stage guards, who urged them on, moving aside the cordons that kept fans away from the stage. Were they in trouble? She didn't want to miss a moment of the show — not after everything she'd done to bring back the Black Cats.

"This way," the security guard said. B gasped as the man lifted her up at the waist and set her on the stage!

Blinding spotlights, screaming fans waving flashlights . . . B stopped in her tracks. It was an ocean of people! Talk about stage fright. Trina smiled and waved them over. B couldn't move. George prodded her from behind. Trina danced over and grabbed B's and George's hands and led them to center stage.

"But they're no match for street cats, who bare their claws and YOWL, yowl, yowl. . . ."

Trina cupped a hand over her headset microphone. "Thanks, guys, for everything."

B inched away, but Trina roped her back in. She put an arm around each of them. Together they all belted out, *"Night's the hour for keeping secrets. But us Cats don't want no secrets, want the whole wide world to hear us YOWL!"*

B's charmed adventures continue in

Read on for a sneak peek!

"Pinch me, B."

Beatrix Cicely, called B for short, looked in surprise at her best friend, George, who had pulled back his sleeve and thrust his arm out in front of her.

"Seriously. Pinch me! I must be dreaming. There's no other possible explanation for today."

B gave George's arm a harmless pinch. "Don't be silly, George! I told you that sooner or later, my dad would let you have a tour of Enchanted Chocolates. It was just a matter of time."

George leaned back in Mr. Cicely's office chair and spun around. He inhaled, long and deep. "Just smell that chocolate!" He sat up and pointed at B. "I'll bet I buy more Enchanted Chocolates than anybody else in the world. I'll bet I do. That makes me their number one customer."

"I don't doubt it," B said, grinning at her friend. She tossed a dart at the dartboard on the wall. It had the logo for Pluto Candies, her father's biggest competitor, taped right at the center of the bull's-eye. She missed. "Thanks for keeping my dad's job secure."

George looked out the window onto the large factory room where workers packed cases of candy. "There goes a truckload of Caramelicious Cremes. And that lady? She's loading a pallet full of Mint Fizzes. That guy's got Peanut Butter Pillows." George slumped down in the office chair. "Oh, man. I'm in heaven."

"No, you're in my chair," B's dad said, entering at just that moment. "C'mon, George. If you think the pallet loading's good, you haven't seen anything yet. You, too, B. I've got a surprise for you both."

They followed Mr. Cicely down the corridor onto an elevator. George tugged on his sleeve. "Wanna hear my idea for what your next new chocolate should be? You'll love this."

"Actually, today . . ."

"It's a candy bar. You start with a simple, flat cracker base. A rectangle. Then you coat it with a layer of peanut brittle. See what I mean? A nice, crunchy, sweet layer of peanut brittle. Drizzle a little caramel over that, then dunk it in chocolate."

"Thanks George, I . . ." B could tell her dad had other things on his mind. But then he paused.

"Wait. Did you say, peanut brittle over a cracker?"

George nodded.

"With caramel? Then chocolate?"

"That's right." George's chest was sticking out a mile.

The elevator doors opened, and they stepped out onto a shiny new wing of the factory that B had never seen before. Her dad was still mentally forming that new candy bar. His voice sounded far away. "The perfect combination of salty and sweet . . . crunchy and smooth . . . And nobody else has done it yet." He whipped out his Crystal Ballphone — any nonwitch would think it was a cell phone — and started punching buttons with his thumbs.

"What're you doing, Dad?" B asked.

"Just texting myself a note to have the kitchens try this out." He finished and snapped the phone shut, then ruffled George's hair. "Keep it under your hats, okay, guys? I may have to put you on the payroll, George."

B feared her friend might faint with happiness. "Better not," she said. "He'd eat sweets all day long.

After a couple of weeks, you'd have to roll him out the door."

They came to a door, and B's dad swiped a pass-card, which let them through. A second door, moments later, required a numeric code, and a third scanned his fingerprint.

"Where are you taking us, to meet the president?" George asked.

"Better than that," Mr. Cicely said. He lowered his voice to a whisper. "You will both get to see the dipping debut for our brand-new, top secret line of chocolates." He paused for impact.

George shook his head in wonder. "This is a day to remember for the rest of my *life*."

Read them all!

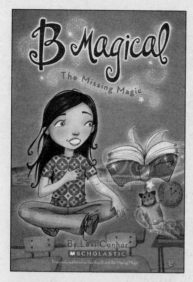

They'll put a S-P-E-L-L on you!